THE KOOKABURRA GAMBIT

Claire McNab

Other Bella Books by Claire McNab

Under the Southern Cross
Silent Heart
Writing My Love

Carol Ashton Series
Lessons in Murder
Fatal Reunion
Death Down Under
Cop Out
Dead Certain
Body Guard
Double Bluff
Inner Circle
Chain Letter
Past Due
Set Up
Under Suspicion
Death Club
Accidental Murder
Blood Link
Fall Guy
Lethal Care

Denise Cleever Series
Murder Undercover
Out of Sight
Recognition Factor
Death by Death
Murder at Random

Kylie Kendall Series
The Wombat Strategy
The Kookaburra Gambit
The Quokka Question
The Dingo Dilemma
The Platypus Ploy

About the Author

Claire McNab is the author of the Detective Inspector Carol Ashton and the Undercover Agent Denise Cleever series. Like the star of her new series, Kylie Kendall, Claire left her native Australia to live in Los Angeles...a city she still finds quite astonishing.

THE KOOKABURRA GAMBIT

Claire McNab

Bella
BOOKS

2015

Bella Books, Inc.
P.O. Box 10543
Tallahassee, FL 32302

First Published 2005 Alyson Publications
First Bella Books Edition 2015

Cover Desginer: Sandy Knowles
ISBN: 978-1-59493-468-1

Acknowledgment

Deep gratitude to Angela Brown, my crash-hot editor!

for Sheila—still musing

CHAPTER ONE

"G'day." The lanky bloke in the Akubra hat and khaki shirt and pants pumped my hand up and down. "I reckon you're Kylie Kendall. Your cousin, Brucie, said to look you up. Said you've aced private-eyeing and are deadset the only one to help us with our little prob."

The second bloke, absolutely identical to the first, nodded. "Yeah," he said.

Behind the desk, Melodie, Kendall & Creeling's receptionist—when she wasn't off auditioning—flashed a dazzling smile. "You're Aussies, aren't you? And twins!"

"Blood oath!" said the first one, obviously taken with Melodie's wide green eyes, blond hair, and perfect teeth. "I'm Alf Hartnidge, and this handsome brute's my brother, Chicka."

Blushing, Chicka bobbed his head.

"Nice little place you've got here," said Alf, looking around the reception area. The floor was red tiles, and there were a couple of hefty earthenware pots, each containing a large cactus bristling with spikes. I'd done a bit of sprucing up around the building—the little fountain in the courtyard now sprouted recycled water enthusiastically, instead of its former depressed dribbling—but I hadn't got to reception yet.

"What do you think of the cacti?" I asked.

Myself, I'd never been fond of such plants. They strike me as rather passive-aggressive, squatting in their pots with their spikes to the ready. To be fair, I had to admit it wasn't their fault they didn't appeal to me, and they did fit in with the pseudo-Spanish style of the building.

Tilting their heads at the exact same angle, Alf and Chicka regarded the contents of the earthenware pots. As they were identical twins, I expected them to look pretty much alike, but it was disconcerting to hear the same voice and see matching body language from two separate people.

Chicka put an exploratory finger out to touch one of the spikes.

"They're sharp;" warned Melodie.

Challenged, Chicka tested this advice. "Ow," he said, sucking his finger. He glared at the cactus.

"I like 'em," said Alf. "Cactuses are survivors"—he tapped himself on the chest—"like the Hartnidges." His expression darkened. "Which brings me to why we're here. Brucie said you were the one to see."

"My cousin recommended me?" I'd been sworn enemies with Brucie, my astringent Aunt Millie's only son, practically from birth. I hadn't seen him for years, and perhaps he'd changed in his loathing for me. I thought it unlikely.

"Brucie did," said Alf in a positive tone. "Spoke highly of you. Told us you'd lobbed over to L.A. to become a private eye. And we need one of those, quick smart. Some lowlife scum is setting us up."

I'd inherited fifty-one percent of my dad's PI company, Kendall & Creeling, but I'd only been a trainee private eye for a few weeks. "It's a bit early in my career to take on a case," I pointed out.

Alf looked stricken. "Fair go, Kylie. You've got to help us. It's opals, you see. And you'd know all about them, coming from

Wollegudgerie." He took off his hat, revealing thick brown hair that seemed to have been hacked with a pair of blunt scissors.

Turning the hat in his hands, he went on, "Ask Chicka. We're up the proverbial creek without a paddle, if you don't help us."

"Yeah," said Chicka. "Up shit creek." He shot an agonized look at Melodie. "Sorry, love. Excuse my French."

His apology got a tinkle of laughter from Melodie—she'd been practicing this laugh for an upcoming audition until everyone in the office had been driven mad. "You're real funny," she said to him.

He ducked his head. "Thanks."

Ariana Creeling, my business partner in Kendall & Creeling Investigative Services, chose this moment to come through the front door. She was her usual cool self, dressed entirely in black and with her sleek blond hair pulled back from her face.

"Good morning," she said briskly, and went on by, her high-heeled boots making exclamations down the tiled hall.

Alf looked after her, his lips set in a silent whistle. "Strewth," he finally said, "did you get those *eyes*?"

I knew what he meant. They had the same effect on me. Ariana had blue eyes of laser-like intensity. In my more poetic moments, I thought of them as glowing with blue fire. Of course, I kept these moments strictly to myself.

"My partner," I said. "Ariana Creeling."

"True?" Alf grinned, then his smile faded. "Pity she's a Yank. She wouldn't know anything about opals, would she?"

"Or kookaburras," said Chicka.

I was rapidly getting out of my depth. "Perhaps you'd better come along to my office."

"I've shut Julia Roberts in there," said Melodie. "She's been annoying Lonnie."

"She does it on purpose," I said, irritated. "She knows he's allergic."

Alf and Chicka looked at each other. "Julia Roberts is in your office?" They spoke in unison.

I repressed a smile. "She is. Come and meet her."

Chicka picked up what looked like a large hiking backpack and slung it over his shoulder. The two of them followed me down the hall.

My office door was like the others in the building, studded with fat brass buttons. "Spanish look," I said, opening it and ushering them in. Ensconced on one of the chairs, Julia Roberts yawned and stretched, then sat up to regard the intruders with her patented blank stare.

"It's a cat," said Alf, his disappointment plain.

"She really belongs to Melodie, but since Melodie's temporarily staying in an apartment building that doesn't take pets, Jules stays here with me."

"You live here?" asked Chicka, winning Julia Roberts's grudging approval by gently stroking her tawny back with appropriate reverence.

"This building used to be a house before it was converted to offices. There's a guest bedroom at the back."

Bob Verritt put his angular head through the door. "Hi," he said. "I heard Kylie had company."

Like Ariana, Bob was a licensed private investigator, and I was, in effect, his apprentice. To become a licensed private eye I had to do two thousand hours of supervised work in the field each year for three years. Six thousand in all. It was a quelling thought, considering I had only accumulated a few hundred so far.

"Come in, Bob," I said. "Meet Alf and Chicka Hartnidge." Although I still had no idea what had brought the twins to Kendall & Creeling, I added, "They've got a problem we might be able to help them with."

They all did the ceremonial shaking-hands bit, Bob hiding rather well his surprise at two identical blokes wearing identical clothes, down to their brown pull-on ankle boots.

The Aussies were tall, but Bob was taller. He had rounded shoulders and was so thin his clothes—he favored navy blue suits—hung on him loosely, looking as though any strong breeze would make them flap like dark blue flags. Bob wasn't the slightest bit handsome, but his face reflected the outstandingly pleasant person he was. He had straight, no-particular-color hair; a strong, hooked nose; and a crooked smile.

"What's the story?" Bob asked.

Alf jerked his head in his brother's direction. "Chicka will show you."

Chicka obediently grabbed the backpack and upended it over my desk. Stuffed toys rained down—all Australian native animals. I saw platypuses, frilled lizards, kangaroos, even a wombat.

"Meet the Oz Mob," said Alf, surveying the toys with pride. "No doubt you've heard of them."

"I'm afraid not," said Bob.

I chimed in with, "News to me too."

Clearly amazed, Chicka said, "You haven't heard of our top-rating kid's TV show, *The Oz Mob*? It's won awards?"

"Sorry."

Chicka clicked his tongue at our ignorance. "*The Oz Mob*'s big at home," he said. "Very big."

"And if all goes well," said Alf, "it'll be gigantic over here in the States."

"If all goes well?" said Chicka, shaking his head mournfully. "If all goes well."

CHAPTER TWO

Bob Verritt and I were sitting in Ariana's office. The room was like her: cool and contained, with a predilection for black, at least in the furniture—black desk, black filing cabinets, black lounge chairs for clients. The walls were flat white. The only break from this stark decor was found in the muted earth colors of a couple of rugs on the polished, dark floor.

"Alf and Chicka are coming back tomorrow," I said. "I told them by then we'd know if we'd be taking the case...or not."

I was dead keen that Kendall & Creeling did take on the Hartnidges as clients, and even keener to be directly involved myself. Not only would the case bump up my total hours, it involved something in which I had expertise. I might know next to nothing about being a private investigator, but I knew just about everything to do with opals. This wasn't surprising, since Mum's pub, The Wombat's Retreat, was smack bang in the middle of Wollegudgerie, premier opal-mining town in outback Australia.

On the other side of the desk, Ariana leaned forward in her chair to examine the three soft toys lying in a neat line in front of her, each with its little belly split open. She picked one up but nearly dropped it when the movement activated its voice.

"I'm Kelvin Kookaburra," the toy bird shrieked. Then it went into peal after peal of maniacal laughter, only stopping when Ariana hastily put it down.

"That's why a kookaburra's also called a laughing jackass," I said helpfully. "They're a type of kingfisher. My aunt lost a lot of goldfish that way, until she put netting over her goldfish pond."

Realizing I was yakking on, I made a mental note to shut up. When I was stressed I tended to talk too much, and Ariana had a talent for making me feel tense. Sure, I'd inherited from my American father a controlling interest in Kendall & Creeling Investigative Services, but for all intents and purposes it was Ariana's company. I was just an Aussie who'd inconveniently turned up and thrown a spanner in the works.

After the first frosty reception, when she'd been gobsmacked to learn I was planning to help run the place, Ariana had warmed to me to some degree—a certain kiss was still burning in my memory—but the uneasy feeling remained that if I said to her I was willing to sell my share, she'd take it like a shot.

I wrenched my attention back to hear Bob saying, "Alf and Chicka Hartnidge have quite a story to tell."

Ariana smiled. "Clearly. Let's have it."

I always melted a bit when she smiled, though I fought to make sure she never knew it. Putting on an alert expression, I gazed at Bob, waiting for him to sum up the Hartnidge brothers' dilemma.

"It's really Kylie's case," he said, "so she should tell you."

Ariana and Bob both looked at me. I cleared my throat. I'd be succinct, to the point, short and snappy, like Ariana would be if she were explaining the situation.

I marshaled my thoughts and began. "Alf and Chicka Hartnidge started off producing a kids' series for Aussie television called *The Oz Mob*, using puppets a bit like the Muppets but based on native animals, such as echidnas, wallabies, and koalas."

"What's an echidna?" said Bob, throwing me off my stride completely.

I glared at him. "Eats insects, gots lots of spines, rolls up in a ball when scared."

"Like a hedgehog?"

"Most likely. Anyway, where was I? Yes, this kids' series turned out to be a mega hit, and Alf and Chicka got the bright idea of licensing someone to make soft toys and hand puppets based on the Oz Mob characters. Soon they were selling like hotcakes—Penny Platypus, Ferdie Frilled Lizard, Korinne Koala, and so on." I indicated the toys on the desk. "But the most popular character of all was that one, Kelvin Kookaburra, probably because he and his mad laugh started and ended the TV show."

Back home, I'd always liked hearing kookaburras laughing. They were impressive birds, with large beaks, square heads, pale downy breasts, and lovely mottled brown-and-blue markings on their backs and wings.

When I was a little kid, I remember being disappointed to learn from my mum that kookas weren't laughing because they had a good sense of humor. It was really: "Get out! This is my area!" Still, they were so handsome I found it easy to forgive them.

"After *The Oz Mob* was a hit," I continued, "it was picked up by a cable channel here in the States, and now it looks like it's going to be a success all over again. There were no flies on the Hartnidge brothers, as far as bargaining was concerned. They licensed the program to television but kept the rights to the soft toys and puppets themselves. Their plan is to import them for sale once the series takes off."

Bob pointed to the three little Kelvin Kookaburra bodies. "Those were in the first shipment." Like a magician, he whipped a velvet bag out of his pocket. "And concealed in them were"—dramatic pause, while he opened the bag and gently spilled the contents onto the desk in front of Ariana—"these!"

These were twenty-eight high-grade opals. Beautiful gems. Each stone was cut and polished, ready to be made into jewelry.

Between us, Bob and I had used the best part of a box of tissues to clean them. They'd been coated in some sort of grease—probably Vaseline—before being hidden inside the Kelvin Kookaburras.

Ariana picked up one of the stones and examined it closely. "Kylie, you must know something about opals."

"Just everything," I said immodestly. "You don't grow up in the 'Gudge without learning every last thing about them."

Bob picked a stone too, holding it to the light pouring in through the skylight. "These are so much more impressive than the opals I've seen here in the States."

"They're certainly not the pale, wishy-washy ones you're used to," I said. "This sort are pretty well only found in Australia. Back home, when people say black opal, they think Lightning Ridge, but I happen to believe Wollegudgerie's stuff is equal, if not better."

Ariana turned the stone in her fingers, and the colors flashed brilliantly. "Why are they called black opals?" she asked. "This one's green and blue."

After weeks of being a novice PI, and not sure what in the hell I was doing most of the time, I was pleased to have a chance to show off my knowledge.

"The name black opal comes from the black potch—the dark layers that provide a terrific contrasting background for the bars of color. That's what makes black opals worth so much more than the milky ones that have white or gray potch." I had to smile, hearing myself. "I'm a regular little mine of information, aren't I?"

"And the value of this little collection?" Ariana asked.

"Worth a motza, because they're solid stones, not doublets or triplets." I picked up another opal, a gorgeous thing shot with fire. "If you look at this from the side, you'll see it's solid stone, not a doublet or triplet."

"Which are?"

"Sometimes very thin opals are attached to a layer of dark opal potch or dark plastic. That makes a doublet. If a clear capping of crystal quartz is put on top as well, it's a triplet. Of course, laminated opals like that aren't as valuable."

Ariana looked thoughtful. "I take it these are all solid stones?"

"They're fair dinkum."

"Could you put a value on them?"

A sharp knock at the door was followed by Fran's entry with Ariana's mail. Fran was Ariana's niece, a fact she took to mean she could show her true personality without worrying about repercussions. This meant she was, as usual, scowling. It was Fran's nature, I'd discovered, to be caustic. She met life with a heavy frown, daring it to confirm her worst suspicions.

Fran's gloomy moodiness didn't go with her looks. She wasn't tall, had red hair, blue eyes—not a patch on Ariana's—and pale skin, plus a truly spectacular bust. To my mind, someone brimming with angst like Fran should be tall and emaciated, with masses of black hair falling over tortured dark eyes.

"Mail," growled Fran. She slapped the envelopes down in the in-box. Then the pile of opals got her fascinated attention. "Wow! Going into the jewelry business, are we?"

"Not likely," I said. "These are shonky goods."

"Contraband," said Bob. "Smuggled into the country."

Fran picked up a stone and examined it. "Lovely." Her scowl had entirely disappeared. Opals clearly had more power than I'd imagined. She looked at me quite civilly. "Your hometown is famous for these, isn't it?"

"Wollegudgerie flame opals, they call them."

Ariana sat back in her chair. "Kylie was about to tell us what these are worth."

"I wouldn't call myself an expert at valuations," I demurred.

"Just go for it," Bob said.

"Opals are valued on depth of color, number of colors, the perfection of the stone, and unique patterns or features," I said. "Just a quick look at this lot shows me these are bonzer—some of the best I've seen. I'd guess they'd be worth at least fifty, sixty thousand. And that's in Australia. Black opals are so rare in the States, they'd fetch quite a lot more. Maybe double."

Bob Verritt looked at the pile of stones with more respect. "The duty on these would be quite a sum. Any way to tell where they were mined?"

"Almost certainly somewhere in Australia—probably Lightning Ridge or Wollegudgerie. We Aussies pretty well have the black opal market tied up and control how much gets exported. That's why this type is so valuable."

I considered mentioning the robbery of Ralphie Bates's Opalarium back in Wollegudgerie, but somehow that wouldn't be fair—not until I'd got the full story out of Alf and Chicka.

"I guess this has something to do with the twin brothers I overheard Melodie babbling on about," said Fran. "She was telling someone on the phone they were so alike it was creepy."

Obviously the receptionist network had been activated. "The Hartnidge brothers," I said. "Alf and Chicka."

"If they've got nothing to do with the smuggling, why don't they go to the authorities and say, 'Gee, fellas, look what we found' and be done with it?"

"Lamb White," said Bob.

Fran frowned, then comprehension dawned. "Lamb White, the Christian movie company? These guys have a deal with them?"

"Pending," said Bob. "And if a breath of anything illegal gets out, the deal's canned."

"Best not to mention a movie company to Melodie," said Ariana.

Fran actually laughed—cynically, of course. "Fat chance you'll keep that little item from her. I'll guarantee she'll sniff it out."

CHAPTER THREE

After Fran left, Ariana, Bob, and I discussed the matter further, and to my delight it was decided we'd go ahead with the case. "From the Hartnidges' point of view, we'll call it your case, Kylie," said Ariana, "but don't forget you're under Bob's strict supervision."

Her subtle emphasis on "strict" deeply irritated me. "Fair go," I said. "You know I won't make a single move without checking first."

Bob grinned. "Like last time?"

He had me there. I'd got myself into a real pickle with an earlier investigation right after I'd arrived in L.A. "I've learnt my lesson," I said.

Ariana's mouth quirked, but she didn't say anything. Bob chuckled.

"I *have*," I said firmly. "True."

While Ariana put the opals in the safe and Bob went off to ring Alf and Chicka to tell them Kendall & Creeling would take the case, I hoofed it to the reception area to ask Melodie for her advice.

Thing was, I needed a haircut. Last time I'd had one was back at Wollegudgerie's only beauty salon, run by Maria, who'd taken up with my girlfriend, Raylene, and broken my heart in the process. This alone had turned me off hairdressers in general.

This morning, however, when I was cleaning my teeth, I noticed how my head looked like it had exploded. I've always had strong hair—as my mum says, it has body to burn—but there's a point where I start to look like one of those supershaggy dogs who spends life peering through a screen of hair.

When I got to reception, Melodie was on the phone. "And even if he is Australian, he's real nice. And Tiffany—get this! He's swinging a deal with Lamb White…Yeah, the goody-two-shoes movie company. And if I play my cards right—" She broke off as she saw me. "Tiff? Call you back, OK?"

"How did you hear about Lamb White?" I asked.

Melodie gave an airy wave with one hand. "Oh, around…"

"You've been listening in."

Melodie's perfectly arched eyebrows drew themselves into an aggrieved frown. "I *never* listen in. I may catch a word now and then." Her expression lightened. "Anyhow, Chicka Hartnidge told me himself. He called to ask me on a date."

"Blimey, he's a fast mover," I observed. Chicka Hartnidge and Melodie Schultz—stage name, Davenport—was a combination to boggle at.

"Chicka said I was a bonzer sheila." Melodie looked at me intently. "That's good, isn't it?"

"Bonzer means excellent, and a sheila's a woman, so I reckon you could say that was pretty good."

She nodded complacently. "I thought so."

"Melodie," I said, "I need some help."

"With what?" She was suspicious. Like, maybe I was going to ask her to do some *work*.

"It's about my hair."

Melodie leaned back to take me in from head to toe. "That's the least of it," she said. "Frankly, Kylie, you need *Extreme Makeover*."

Fran came tootling along in time to hear this last observation. She looked me up and down too. "I hardly ever agree with Melodie on anything," she said, "but this time she's right."

"Are you fair dinkum? I'm not that far gone, am I?"

Melodie and Fran looked at each other, then at me. "How can we count the ways?" Fran asked.

"OK, I admit I haven't got anorexia, and I do need a haircut pretty desperately, but otherwise I don't look too bad, do I?"

"Hmmm," said Fran, folding her arms. "What do you think, Melodie?"

"Hard to know where to begin."

While they had a little giggle about that, I tried to be absolutely objective about myself. Mum, being part Aborigine, had given me her dark hair, deep brown eyes, and olive skin. My dad's genes had passed on my height, my hands, and my quite elegant nose and squarish chin.

I thought of Ariana, what she must see when she looked at me. An outback sheila, rough 'round the edges, who'd made foot-in-mouth her second name. It wasn't that I hadn't had a good education—I'd aced it at Wollegudgerie High—but no one would call me sophisticated, especially not by L.A. standards.

"OK," I said to Melodie and Fran. "I'm yours."

* * *

Two hours later, there I was in the professional clutches of Luigi of Beverly Hills, or would be any minute. We'd hardly met before his cell phone went off, playing the first few bars of the overture to *The Barber of Seville*. Now Luigi was deep in a conversation that required him to march up and down, making many sweeping hand gestures.

I looked around. The beauty salon was long and narrow, with mirrors down both walls. Facing the mirrors were a multitude of hairdressing chairs. I'd never seen so many in one place.

Crikey, Wollegudgerie's Snip & Slather beauty salon looked like a broom cupboard next to this one. The place was filled with loud techno music, almost drowning out the constant noise of people coming and going, screaming "Dahling!" and air-kissing, or, as I soon discovered, recounting in astonishing detail very private crises in their lives.

I became entranced by the blond woman sitting in the chair next to me. Her hairdresser, a large bloke with very tight curly black hair, who answered to the name Albert, was hard at work eliminating her dark roots. While he slapped stuff on her scalp, she gave him the gruesome details about the bizarre sexual favors her life coach had demanded.

"My God!" exclaimed her hairdresser. "I call that sexual harassment."

"Sexual harassment?" the blond said. "That's not my complaint. The SOB was just no good in the sack."

Albert gave a cry of commiseration. "Major disappointment."

Before I could hear more, Luigi, tall, thin, and with an almost unruly head of silver hair—I reckoned he was going for a Greek-godish look—finished his call and came to stand behind the chair. We both regarded my reflection in the mirror.

"By luck I had a last-minute cancellation," Luigi said. He was in his fifties, I reckoned, but fit with it, and had a charming Italian accent. "Melodie made it clear it was an emergency." He shook his silver head. "She didn't exaggerate."

"It's that bad?"

He lifted a chunk of hair, held it out from my head for a few moments, then let it drop. Sighing, he asked, "My dear! Who is responsible for this?"

"I suppose I am."

Plainly horrified, he stared at me in the mirror. I expected him to cross himself any moment. At last he got out, "You styled it yourself?"

"Of course not. But it's been a while since I had a haircut. I've been putting it off."

"We don't have our hair *cut*." Luigi's tone was severe. "We have it *styled*."

"Fair enough. It's been a while since I had my hair *styled*."

After he examined more strands closely, his lips tightened as if in pain. "What conditioner do you use?"

"I don't use a conditioner. I just wash my hair."

Luigi closed his eyes. "I see." He rallied to say, "You must promise me to never, repeat *never*, let whoever did this to you touch your head again." He clicked his tongue. "Should be a capital offense."

I could have told him there was no way Maria would ever get within cooee of my hair again, not after what she'd done. Oh, I had to be honest. It took two to tango. Maria couldn't have led Raylene astray if Raylene hadn't fancied a tango on the side with someone other than me.

"Marta!" Luigi was beckoning imperiously to a tiny woman in a turquoise smock. "Marta! Over here. Take this woman to the basins!"

He patted my shoulder consolingly. "Put yourself in my hands," he said. "It will take all my skill, but Luigi can repair the damage?"

I knew from what Melodie and Fran had told me it would also take an astonishing amount of dollars. "How much?!" I'd yelped when they'd told me. "Stone the crows! That'd cover years of haircuts back in the 'Gudge."

The two of them had also got me up to speed on the subject of tipping. Back home we didn't tip much—maybe round up the taxi fare to the nearest dollar, or put a bit extra on a restaurant bill—but here in the States it seemed you tipped everybody, all the time.

I checked that I had the tip money in my pocket as I followed Marta's diminutive form to the back of the salon. We passed through the manicuring section, full of people talking nineteen to the dozen while seated opposite each other at tiny tables. My nose twitched at the smell of acetone and nail polish. Melodie had suggested I have my nails painted with her favorite color, Dark Desire, and had even tried to give me a bottle of the stuff to take with me for my manicure. I didn't want to hurt Melodie's feelings, but it really was an awful color, like clotted blood, so

I'd conveniently forgotten to take the bottle with me when I'd left the office.

Marta, with me bringing up the rear, arrived at the washing area, where a row of bright pink basins were set along one wall. All the accompanying chairs were occupied by people with their heads dangling while lather flew. There seemed to be a bit of a traffic jam; three other clients were waiting for a vacant spot. Like in the rest of the salon, everybody was talking extra loud to be heard above the music.

Marta got me a black robe to put on, then hovered like a vulture until one of the chairs freed up. The moment it did, she went in for the kill, beating another turquoise-smocked woman to the punch. "Mine, I believe," said Marta, baring her teeth as she shoved me into the chair.

In a flash she had me where she wanted me. As she hit one lever to drop the back, and another to raise a support under my legs, the chair immediately became an instrument of torture, stretching me out helpless on my back, with my neck in what felt like plastic vice and my head hanging over the basin.

"Comfortable?" Marta inquired.

"Not really."

Marta didn't hear me, her attention being caught by the conversation at the washing station beside us. "A breast lift that went tragically wrong," the woman washing the hair of a fellow victim was saying. "Poor thing's quite lopsided."

My neck was immovable, but I rolled my eyes to see who was speaking. Oddly, as well as her turquoise smock, the woman wore a wide-brimmed hat.

"And he's supposed to be the best plastic surgeon in Beverly Hills!" exclaimed Marta.

"I've heard he's a pig," said the hatted woman's client.

"Really?" said Marta. "Where did you hear that?"

"At a fund-raiser for Afghanistan orphans. Deanna Dorrell was at the same table. Had an *awful* time with him, she was saying."

"Face-lift? I thought she looked tight around the eyes in her last photo."

"Botox only." The client sniffed. "Of course, they *all* say that."

Belatedly, Marta remembered me. "Comfortable?"

An industrial-strength blast of water spared my need to reply. "Too hot?" Marta inquired.

"Well…"

"Good."

Marta might be little, but crikey, she had hands that could tear a phone book in half. I squeezed my eyes shut as she vigorously massaged, wondering if she might actually rip my scalp from my head. Scalped in a Beverly Hills hairdressing salon? I was just imagining how I'd break the news to Mum when Marta hit me with the water again.

"Conditioner?"

Bearing in mind Luigi's shock that I didn't use such a thing, I said, "Good-oh."

"That a yes?"

"Yes."

More violent massaging. My neck was breaking, my ears were ringing, I was vowing this was the last time I'd go through this hell, when Marta announced, "There you go."

Abruptly I was returned to an upright position. Marta fixed me with a cheerful smile as she deftly wound a white towel around my head. I fumbled in my pocket and found the folded dollars. I'd erred on the generous side after Melodie and Fran had told me how much to tip the hair washer—maybe too much, as Marta's smile became quite manic.

"Next time," she said, tenderly dabbing a stray drop of water on my face, "ask for me."

Back at the station, Luigi was on the phone again, shouting in Italian—a language I knew a bit about because I'd done a course in conversational Italian. I wasn't awfully good at it, and Italian-Australians had been known to snigger at my accent, but I'd persevered, and as long as people spoke slowly, I could understand quite a bit.

Luigi appeared to be arguing with someone about the installation of a toilet suite in his apartment, but he spoke so fast I couldn't be sure. After a final yell, he slapped his little cell phone shut, snarling a few harsh words that definitely hadn't been included in my curriculum.

As he caught sight of me standing there, his expression changed to one of resolution. Then he forced a smile. "Come," he said. "Your transformation begins."

CHAPTER FOUR

Feeling light-headed, in more ways than one, I reclaimed my generic rental sedan from a nearby parking structure. The notice at the entrance proclaimed FIRST TWO HOURS FREE! but my mini makeover had taken rather longer than that, so I had to pay on my way out.

Although I'd only been in L.A. a few weeks, I'd already found driving in the shopping area of Beverly Hills held particular challenges. Herds of tourists, necks hung with cameras, wandered along, eyeballing all the famous retailers, no doubt hoping to see a celebrity popping into Gucci or being ushered out of Giorgio Armani.

I'd discovered tourists had to be watched closely. Apparently bemused by the heady influence of the conspicuous consumption surrounding them, they often wandered off the footpath and onto the roadway, or crossed against DON'T WALK signals.

Things were made even more interesting by the drivers of luxury cars and fat SUVs. I wished I could multitask like they did. It seemed child's play for Beverly Hills denizens to negotiate the crowded streets, all without actually running into another vehicle or mowing down a tourist, at the same time carrying on an animated cell phone conversation, spying a rare parking spot, ignoring the furious horns of inconvenienced motorists, and reversing into the spot.

When I ground to a halt outside Yves Saint Laurent I realized I'd made a poor decision to use Rodeo Drive to get to Santa Monica Boulevard. Rodeo was so clogged with traffic, vehicular and human, that I was doomed to stop-start, with a predominance of stop, all the way. However, this did give me opportunities to steal looks at my new hairstyle in the rearview mirror. Of course I'd seen myself in the salon, but now that I was out in the real world I wanted to reassure myself my initial impressions were right and that people wouldn't break into helpless laughter when they saw the new me.

The mirror being small, and my head quite large, I had to rotate this way and that to build up a visual jigsaw of my hairdo. I had to hand it to Luigi—I did look different.

He'd spent ages evaluating, lips pursed, before seizing his scissors and beginning to cut infinitesimal amounts off here, there, and everywhere. It took forever. He snip-snip-snipped until I got restive, then he blow-dried until I got really twitchy, then he snipped some more. I'd been about to whinge that my nether regions had pins and needles, when he'd stood back to admire his work.

"*Bellisimo*," he'd said, crinkling his eyes attractively. He made a sweeping gesture in my direction. "*E' una bella donna!*"

"*Grazie.*"

I'd been told the thing to do was to give Luigi's check and tip to him unobtrusively, but I couldn't see why one had to be underhanded about it, so I gave it to him straight. He slipped it quickly into his pocket without even looking.

"What if I haven't paid you enough?" I said.

He gave me a big grin. "In that case, I'll have your legs broken."

I smiled back. Of course he was joking, but then again, he *was* Italian.

Then it had been Perdita's turn to have a lash at improving me. She was one of the manicurists I'd passed on my way to the basins. Perdita wore a pink smock and had a disturbingly intense stare. She sat knee to knee with me, the tiny manicure table between us, and turned her piercing gaze onto my fingernails. I held my breath. I had a nasty feeling the verdict would not be good.

Perdita peered more closely. Then she blinked rapidly. It was only a minor version of Luigi's horror at the state of my hair, but I felt defensive anyway. "I've never had a professional manicure," I said.

Perdita had been too polite to announce this regrettable fact was obvious, but her expression had said it for her.

"I've got good, strong nails," I'd announced, as if this might excuse the inexcusable.

"Your cuticles!" Perdita's face had contained a mixture of revulsion and grief. She'd shaken her head. "Your cuticles..."

Now, stuck at yet another red light, this time outside Cartier, I snuck a look at my hands. My cuticles were exemplary. It'd been a battle, but I'd persuaded Perdita I didn't want nail polish, even the clear stuff. Hiding her contempt, she'd buffed my nails furiously, until they shone.

Something was ringing. I was puzzled for a moment, then realized it was my mobile. Making a mental note to call it a cell phone like Americans did, I flipped it open.

Chantelle said in a rush, "Kylie? How did it go? Do you look totally adorable?"

I didn't ask how Chantelle knew where I'd been. Back at the office, Melodie had tapped into the amazing outreach of the receptionists' network. Possibly thousands of people in L.A. were now aware I'd recently challenged the creative abilities of Luigi of Beverly Hills.

"Doesn't look too bad," I conceded.

Chantelle chuckled. She had a dusky, warm laugh that went with her smooth, dark skin. "This I've got to see. Tonight?"

"Ripper idea!"

Chantelle suggested where and when, and I rang off, cheered because I needed some no-strings-attached romantic action. Lately I'd found myself brooding entirely too much about Ariana Creeling.

From the moment I saw her, I realized Ariana was a woman no one would ever forget. It wasn't her extraordinary blue eyes, startling though they were, or that she was astonishingly beautiful, because although Ariana was attractive, she wasn't clutch-at-your-throat gorgeous. It was something indefinable, perhaps to do with her cool, contained manner and her aura of unattainability.

And yet, just once, she'd kissed me.

* * *

I'd taken so long at the beauty salon, and the traffic on Sunset Boulevard was so jammed, that by the time I got back to the office the parking area was half empty.

Technically, as I was co-owner of Kendall & Creeling Investigative Services, the people who worked there were my staff too, although I was pretty sure none of them thought of me as the boss. After all, I was so green I was apprenticed to Bob Verritt to learn the ropes.

Still, in a sense they *did* work for me, even if Ariana Creeling was clearly in charge, so I checked out who was still there. Ariana's deep-blue BMW was parked in its designated spot. Next to it, a snazzy red convertible indicated Melodie was still more or less manning reception. I noticed Lonnie Moore, who handled everything electronic, including all the latest spy devices, had parked his battered brown Nissan in Fran's spot. Luckily, Fran's oversize SUV wasn't in evidence, or there would have been a nasty scene. Fran was *very* territorial.

Bob Verritt's silver Toyota was missing, as was Harriet Porter's black VW Beetle—the new model, not the lawn mower–engined one on which I'd learnt to drive yonks ago, back in Wollegudgerie. Harriet was working for the company part-time while putting herself through law school. On top of that, she was pregnant. And she still looked like a million dollars. It wasn't really fair.

As I parked my rental car, I thought that soon I'd have to decide whether to buy or lease a vehicle. The alternative was to drive my dad's lovingly restored 1960s Mustang, at present parked in a garage at the rear of the building.

The Mustang was a gorgeous red, and its engine had a wonderful throaty roar, but it wasn't an automatic. In Australia we drive on the other side of the road and change gears with the left hand. I'd tried driving the Mustang in L.A. traffic and had found it more of a challenge than I'd expected, what with shifting gears and staying on the right side of the road at the same time.

Besides, Ariana had pointed out that one of the tasks a PI often faced was tailing someone in traffic. No way could a vehicle like my dad's blend in with other cars. I sighed. It looked like I'd have to get some boring neutral-colored sedan.

I did a final check in my mirror, then, feeling rather self-conscious, got out of the car and headed for the front door, stopping in the middle of the courtyard to check on the fountain. It was spurting water as heartily as one could wish, which was gratifying, as its overhaul had cost rather more than I'd expected.

"Plumbers," Fran had said with bitter scorn as she'd viewed the invoice. "They make more than brain surgeons." She'd fixed me with a beady look. "This was the *lowest* quote?"

"They were the only company that said they were fountain specialists."

"Specialists?" Fran had snarled. "Every Tom, Dick, and Harry's a specialist. Run it by me first, Kylie, before you do anything like this again. After all, I *am* the office manager."

"Right-oh." I'd inwardly smiled. Somewhere along the line, Fran had bestowed the title of office manager upon herself, even though her job was more general assistant, or, as I'd had it explained to me, a gofer.

I took a deep breath. Enough of this shilly-shallying around. I made for the front door.

"Awesome!" exclaimed Melodie, examining me from behind the reception desk. "I love your bangs."

"My what?"

"Bangs." When I still didn't comprehend, she added, "The hair hanging over your forehead, Kylie. Bangs."

"You mean my fringe?"

"I guess so."

I grinned at her. "Back home, you wouldn't say that."

"You Aussies talk real funny," Melodie observed. "So what's a bang? I'd like to know, in case Chicka says it."

That made me laugh. "You'd better know what he means if he uses the word."

"Well? What does it mean?"

"How to put this delicately?" I said. "A bang is...doing it."

Melodie looked at me with delighted astonishment. "You mean...?"

"Yes, going all the way."

"*No!* So every time someone mentions your bangs to you..." She dissolved into giggles.

"I'm afraid so," I said.

Melodie's amusement faded as she noticed my hands. She frowned accusingly at my naked fingernails. "Where's the Dark Desire?"

"Where indeed?" said Lonnie Moore, on his way out. "I ask myself that all the time."

"Oh, *funny*," muttered Melodie. I knew she was down on Lonnie at the moment, because I'd overheard him refusing to cover the phone for her tomorrow morning, when Melodie planned to be off on what seemed to be her ten-thousandth audition.

"Whoa," said Lonnie, getting a gander at my new hairstyle. "What have we here?" He put down his things and circled me with a critical expression on his chubby face. Then he gave me the full blast of his little-boy smile, dimples and all. "Not bad," he said.

I felt myself blush. "Thanks."

My heart gave a skip when I heard the cadence of Ariana's footsteps. She had a graceful, loose-hipped stride that was absolutely unmistakable. She was carrying a briefcase and was obviously in a hurry. She didn't pause, but as she passed me, she put out a finger and brushed my cheek. "Looking good," she said. Then she was gone.

I knew I was blushing even more. "This is embarrassing," I announced, hoping to hide the effect just one light touch had had on me. Hell's bells, if one fingertip could do this, what would...

My imagination short-circuited. Suddenly I became aware that Melodie was flashing a particularly ingratiating smile in my direction.

"Can't do it. Sorry," I said.

Melodie's lower lip shot out. "I haven't asked you for anything yet."

"Oh, but you *will*," said Lonnie, with the weariness of one who knew this from long experience. He was usually sunny-natured, but Melodie had the knack of bringing out his dark side. "Don't fall for it, Kylie. You've been here long enough to know Melodie always says this audition's her One Big Chance." He glared at her. "And you're away for hours and hours, but it never pans out."

"Is this the audition you've been practicing your laugh for?" I asked.

"That's the one." Melodie tinkled a giggle to demonstrate.

"Oh, Jesus!" Lonnie muttered.

"I'll look after the phone for you," I said with a noble expression, "but only if you swear never to laugh that laugh again."

Put out, Melodie said, "But, Kylie, it's part of my laughter repertoire. An actor must have the full range. Run the gamut—guffaw, chuckle, snigger—"

"Oh, Lord!" Lonnie looked at the ceiling. "Take me now."

"Laughter's real subtle," snapped Melodie. "Not that you'd appreciate that, Lonnie. There's a world of difference between a snicker and a hoot, you know."

Lonnie didn't hear her, having caught sight of Julia Roberts, who, tail erect, was making a beeline for him. "Get away from me, cat!"

I was convinced it amused Jules to inflame Lonnie's allergies. "You're only encouraging her," I said. It was obvious Lonnie didn't understand feline psychology. "The more you reject Julia Roberts, the more she wants to be with you."

"I'm outta here," said Lonnie, grabbing his things and skipping through the front door before Julia Roberts could get to him.

"Don't worry, Jules," I said, stroking her. "I love you."

"I was wondering about that," said Melodie. "See, Kylie, it's like this. Lexus has asked me to move in with her permanently. And you know her apartment building has a rule against pets. Do you mind if Julia Roberts stays here with you?"

"You mean for good?"

Melodie nodded hopefully. "Uh-huh."

"All right," I said, secretly chuffed. I get on well with cats because I acknowledge their superiority immediately. They like that. "You're flatting with someone called Lexus? I thought her name was Cathy."

"Cathy's *so* commonplace. She decided to change it to something more exclusive."

"Rather like a luxury car?" I said.

"Well, yes."

"You're not thinking of changing your name to Mercedes, are you?" I had a bit of a grin at that. "Or what about Porsche or Ferrari?"

She didn't smile. "Larry, my agent, says Melodie Davenport is the perfect name for me."

I found it quite endearing that Melodie always referred to Larry Argent as "Larry, my agent." It was obviously a point of pride for an actor to have an agent, even if she never got any acting work. I'd never set eyes on the man. Maybe he didn't even exist, but if he did, he'd be pleased to know his name was constantly on Melodie's lips.

"This agent of yours," I said. "Has anyone here ever met him?"

"Quip knows Larry, my agent," Melodie said. Quip was Fran's husband, a top bloke.

I was going to ask more, but Melodie was feverishly gathering up various shopping bags she had hidden under the desk. "Gotta go, Kylie. I'm running late. Thanks for looking after things tomorrow morning. I'll be in as soon as I can."

She paused at the door. "Oh, there was a message for you. Your mom called."

"Did she say why?"

Melodie gave an airy wave. "Something about a wombat in crisis." She looked back over her shoulder as she opened the door. "She sounded real upset. Said it was urgent."

"Then why did you wait till now to tell me?" I demanded, but Melodie had gone.

I checked my watch. Back in the 'Gudge it would be late morning of the next day. Before calling, I locked the front door and checked that everything in the building was secure. Julia Roberts came with me on my safety patrol. "Looks like it's you and me, Jules," I said to her. "Melodie practically said you were mine."

Julia Roberts gave me a cool look. Cats don't belong to anyone but themselves. "Sorry," I said.

Satisfied we were secure, I headed back to my room to call Mum. Jules came too, although she did linger for a moment or two outside the kitchen. Her philosophy about food was to eat early and often, and it was a source of annoyance to her that I didn't share her views.

"You don't want to be a fat cat," I said. With a vexed snap of her tail she stalked after me.

Along with the fountain and the installation of a laundry alcove off the kitchen, I'd spent a fair amount of money on my bedroom. The cartons of papers and the odd assortment of sports equipment I'd found there had been relocated. I'd kept the queen-size bed with its beaut carved headboard, but I'd got rid of the humongous dresser, which took up too much space, and replaced it with something smaller.

The original bedspread and curtains had had an identical pattern of garish geometric shapes. My new bedspread had soothing shades of blue. The deepest hue was picked up in the thick throw rugs on the polished dark flooring. I'd ditched the curtains altogether and gone for wooden slat blinds.

When I'd first arrived, the television and DVD player in the room had been housed in ugly metal shelving. Now they sat in an elegant wall unit that included a music setup and flat-screen computer. I love books, so I'd had shelves built in. Because I'd left Wollegudgerie with the minimum of luggage, the shelves were pretty well bare, except for a street directory and a how-to book I'd bought, *Private Investigation: The Complete Handbook.* Once Mum calmed down about me living in L.A., I was going to ask her to ship over all my favorite books.

Julia Roberts, being psychic, knew I was going to make myself comfortable on the bed before I called Mum, so of course she immediately plunked herself in the middle of the bedspread and began a complicated full-body wash. I perched on the edge and picked up the phone from the side table. The phone was new too, a deep blue number with lots of buttons for functions I'd never use.

"Mum? It's me."

"Kylie? Where've you been? I rang you hours ago."

"Sorry. I've just got back."

"Back from where?"

"Beverly Hills, actually."

"Beverly Hills? What were you doing there?"

"Nothing important."

Silence. My mum would make an excellent professional interrogator. You couldn't deflect her, no matter how hard you tried. She'd wait you out. It was easier to give in and tell her what she wanted to know. "I had my hair done in a beauty salon. And a manicure."

"That cost a pretty penny, I'd reckon."

I told her how much. She gasped.

Any moment now she'd be telling me how much cheaper haircuts were in Maria's salon in Wollegudgerie. Before Mum could get onto that dangerous topic, I said, "The message you left with Melodie mentioned a wombat crisis. Do you mean there's something wrong at the pub?"

Before I was twenty I was pretty well running the financial side of Mum's hotel, the Wombat's Retreat. Eventually I had all the accounts computerized, I'd built a Web site and had started to link up with travel sites all over the world.

Even with Raylene throwing me over and shredding my heart, I might still be there in the pub, if Mum hadn't fallen in love with Jack O'Connell. It's not that I didn't get on with Jack, but once he and my mum were officially engaged, he started throwing his weight around. It was obvious once they tied the knot, Jack intended to play boss cocky, even if he knew next to nothing about the hotel business.

The situation was enough to get me thinking about leaving the outback and having a go at living in a big city, probably Sydney. Then my dad died. Mum had divorced him when I was a little kid, so he was the American father I hardly knew. You could have knocked me down with a feather when I found he'd left me a chunk of money and his share of Kendall & Creeling.

"Things are crook at the Wombat without you, love," said my mum. "Jack's made a right mess of the accounts. You're needed here, darling. Come home."

"You don't need me, Mum. You need an accountant, that's all. Or a good bookkeeper. Someone who knows the hotel business."

"This is your home, Kylie. I don't want you living thousands of kilometers away from all your friends and family. It's not right."

"Mum, I'm not a child. I'm practically thirty."

"Twenty-eight, last time I looked."

"Speaking of family," I said, "what's my cousin, Brucie, up to these days?"

"Nephew Brucie?"

I grinned. Brucie was Mum's sister's son, and my mum had always irritated the hell out of him by calling him "Nephew Brucie."

"I was wondering, Mum, because it seems Brucie recommended me as a private eye to these two Aussie blokes, Alf and Chicka Hartnidge."

Mum snorted. "I told Nephew Brucie to stop it. Spoke to Millie about it too, not that his mother's ever had the gumption to discipline the boy. From the time he was a baby, he's got away with bloody murder. Spare the rod and spoil the child, I always say."

With misgivings, I asked, "What is it that Brucie has to stop?"

My mum gave another contemptuous snort. "Nephew Brucie's been telling anyone who'll listen that you've made a big splash in the States in the private eye area, and he's going to open your Aussie branch. He says you want him to move to L.A. to learn the business."

"Stone the crows!"

Temporarily silenced by the truly dreadful vision of my cousin lobbing in on me, I only half-listened as Mum went on. "As for Alf and Chicka, you know the family, the Hartnidges of Last Gasp Creek. Of course, the twins aren't at home anymore, but they visit often. There was a big crowd of Hartnidges at the footy final last year, remember?"

"Mum, you've got to make sure Brucie doesn't come to Los Angeles."

"He won't. Don't worry about that." The feeling of relief this gave me dissolved with her next words. "I can't leave the pub in Jack's hands—God knows what he'd get up to—and Nephew Brucie's going nowhere, believe me. So it's all up to Millie."

I got one of those cold feelings you read about in books, where a chill goes down your spine and your hands get clammy. "What's Aunt Millie got to do with it?" I held my breath.

"Someone has to go over there and talk some sense into you, Kylie. Millie and I discussed it last night. She'll be leaving next week."

I opened my mouth, but no words came out. Julia Roberts stopped washing and looked at me with interest.

Aunt Millie was coming to L.A.

Aunt Millie who'd made sarcasm an art form.

Aunt Millie who made a lemon seem sweet.

Aunt Millie, who, unbelievable though it seemed, would make Fran look like Pollyanna.

Aunt Millie!

CHAPTER FIVE

Chantelle was picking me up at eight to take me to Club Jabber, a nightclub that had just opened. Going there was part of my getting-to-know-L.A. campaign. Strewth, half the time I didn't know what people were talking about, and if I were to ace being a PI, I had to know the territory. That meant a crash course in everything, including local nightlife.

I had a quick shower, being careful not to muss my new hairstyle, then made myself a cheese-and-pickle sandwich and a cup of tea to tide me over. I served Julia Roberts tuna. For such an elegant cat, she wasn't what I'd call a delicate eater. She hoed into it like she hadn't had food for days, making rather disgusting slurping noises.

"We chew with our mouths closed in this house," I said, repeating the words my mum had said to me a zillion times when I was growing up. Jules ignored me.

I had some time to kill, so I went back to my room and sat down with *Private Investigation: The Complete Handbook*. I was up to the chapter on how to tell when someone's lying to you.

Liars, I read, tend to touch their mouths or noses when saying something untrue. I was so engrossed, I jumped when the phone rang.

"I'm outside, Kylie," said Chantelle. "And you're not. Where are you?"

"Got caught up in something. Be there in a mo."

I grabbed my things, said goodbye to Julia Roberts, and rushed out the front door. As soon as I appeared in the parking area, Chantelle, who was leaning against her red Jeep, gave my hair the once-over. "I like it." Then she gave the rest of me an up and down, and grinned. "That goes for the rest of you too."

I was wearing one of the outfits Harriet Porter had helped me buy, and if I say so myself, I didn't look too bad. "You're pretty crash-hot, yourself," I said, clambering into the passenger seat.

Chantelle was someone who could wear very bright colors and not be swamped by them. Tonight she looked terrific in an iridescent orange top and pants I would never even try to get away with. Maybe it was the contrast with her dark skin, but more likely it was all to do with the way she walked, her voice, her laugh, her mannerisms. Whatever it was, it added up to a personal style. That got me brooding. I reckoned I didn't have a personal style.

Chantelle glanced across at me. She had a really kissable, pouting red mouth. "What's the matter?"

"Not a thing. How's the new job?" Chantelle had just started as a receptionist at Unified Flair Inc., a talent agency. It had to be a big one, as even I had heard of it.

While Chantelle negotiated Thursday night traffic on Sunset, we chatted about the stars and near-stars and never-will-be stars she'd dealt with in the last few days.

"Delford Gunderson," Chantelle said, "is a sweetie, but I wouldn't give the time of day to Maria Flann."

"Dinkum?" I said, a bit down to hear this. Maria Flann had been one of my fave movie stars for years.

"If that means you're asking me if it's true," said Chantelle, "the answer's yes. Actually, the things I've heard…"

Even if half of what Chantelle then told me was dinky-di, those stars certainly had an interesting time of it. "Does all this stuff get on the receptionist network?" I asked, thinking how much I'd hate to have everything about my life out there for anyone to know.

"Of course not." said Chantelle. "It wouldn't be professional to disclose every detail."

"How do you decide what details you *can* let slip?"

"A receptionist just knows. It's a talent."

Club Jabber was in West Hollywood. As we hit Santa Monica Boulevard, I remembered something I wanted Chantelle to explain. "The woman next to me in the salon this afternoon was talking about her life coach. What's a life coach?"

She grinned. "You sure don't need one, honey!"

"So what does a life coach do?"

"A life coach asks what's missing in your life and what you really want to achieve then gets you to set personal goals. Basically, they keep telling you you're marvelous. It's like having your own private one-person cheer squad."

"People get paid to do this life coaching?"

"Thousands and thousands."

"Beats me why you'd give money to a stranger." I said, "when all you need to do is to sit down and think about it yourself, or maybe talk it out with friends."

"I don't know." said Chantelle, shrugging. "People get in a rut and need someone else to pull them out of it. Quip should be at the club tonight. You can ask him. He was a life coach for a while."

"Quip? Fran's husband? He's a screenwriter."

She laughed indulgently. "Kylie, every second person in this town's a screenwriter. Or an actor. Or both. Then they find you've got to do other things to put food on the table."

I chuckled. "Next you're going to say *you've* got a screenplay."

Chantelle seemed rather miffed by my lighthearted tone. "Actually, yes, I have. A romantic comedy."

"Don't tell me! One of the main characters is a receptionist."

Her eyebrows dived into a V. She was definitely miffed. "Something wrong with that?" she said in an icy voice.

Yerks! I'd better tread carefully. "Nothing wrong with that at all." I had to get off this subject fast. "My Aunt Millie's coming to Los Angeles," I remarked.

"That's nice."

"No, it isn't."

Chantelle had expressive eyebrows. Now they were raised in questioning arcs. "No?"

"It's a disaster. Could hardly be worse."

Chantelle took her eyes off the road to stare at me. "This must be some aunt!"

"She's indescribable. You'd have to meet her to see what I mean. Not that you will." Chantelle's hurt expression spurred me to add hastily, "That didn't come out quite right. It's not just you. *Nobody* is going to meet Aunt Millie, if I have anything to do with it."

Chantelle's disbelief was plain. "And your aunt will be happy with this? Not meeting anyone? What are you going to do? Lock her in a room?"

"If only." I was plunged into gloom. Chantelle was right. Aunt Millie would make it her business to meet everyone who had anything to do with me.

"I've got to meet your Aunt Millie," said Chantelle enthusiastically. "She sounds like a real kick."

"Real kick? Is that something good? If so, it doesn't apply to my aunt."

"She can't be that bad."

I slumped in my seat. "You don't know the half of it."

We turned off the main road onto a narrow laneway. "We have to find somewhere to park," said Chantelle. "Quip said you could usually get something down here."

"How do you know Quip?" Chantelle had never mentioned she'd met Fran's husband before.

"UCLA Writers' Program. We were in the same script-writing course a few years ago, when we were both starting out."

Quip had written what seemed countless scripts for movies and television—not one of them made—but at least he was involved in the biz in some way. As far as I knew, Chantelle had only one screenplay.

"Has your screenplay got a title?" I asked.

Chantelle swore under her breath as someone ahead of us snaffled an empty parking spot. She turned the Jeep into yet another narrow lane. "I was going to call it *Wrong Number*, but then I decided *Sorry, Wrong Number* had more pizzazz."

"Hasn't *Sorry, Wrong Number* already been used?"

Chantelle didn't seem concerned. "Has it? Doesn't matter. There's no copyright with titles."

"So you could call your screenplay *Gone With the Wind* if you wanted to?"

Chantelle shot me a look worthy of Julia Roberts in one of her more haughty moments. "That title wouldn't relate to the essential themes I'm exploring."

I could tell I was getting into chancy territory here. I peered through the windscreen. "Isn't that a parking spot?"

"Where?!"

I pointed. "Someone's just pulling out."

Chantelle accelerated like mad, then slammed on the brakes when we got to the gap in the parked cars. "Get it fast, or lose it," she said, reversing into the space with impressive skill. Thwarted, a guy going the other way gave us the finger as he passed.

We weren't that far from Club Jabber, which was hard to find unless you picked out the tiny red J above the black door. A big bloke was standing outside it, arms folded over his barrel chest. He wore a very tight white T-shirt that carried the words STONE KILLER in that really purple-purple that puts your teeth on edge. There was a small knot of people clustered around him, but he was ignoring their attempts to talk to him.

"Be nice to the bouncer," said Chantelle.

I looked at the bloke with interest. I'd never met a bouncer before, unless you counted Mucka Onslow, who was the sergeant in charge of the cop shop in the 'Gudge but also doubled on the sly as private security for high school dances and the like.

"G'day," I said to him.

The bouncer grunted. Chantelle said, "It's all right, Dana. She's with me."

Without a flicker of expression on his face, he stood aside and let us into the club. There was an annoyed mutter from the people left waiting outside as we disappeared through the black door.

Safely inside, I said, "The bouncer's name is Dana? That's strictly a girl's name where I come from."

"For pity's sake, don't tell Dana that."

I grinned. "You think he'd mind being told he has a girly name?"

"My guess is he'd mind a lot."

The air trembled with the thump-thump of a bass beat. A bored young woman perched on a tall stool behind a pay window set into the wall. She was chewing gum so hard I thought there was a fair chance she might dislocate her jaw.

"My treat," said Chantelle, shoving money through the slot at the bottom of the glass.

We went down a short, dimly lit hallway and through heavy black curtains, where the sound hit us like a slap in the face. My breastbone was actually vibrating, and my eardrums felt like they were bending inward. I reckoned enough of this and I'd be permanently deafened.

All this sound was coming from a band spotlighted on a tiny stage. The lead guitarist, who wore a shocking pink shirt open to the waist and super tight black jeans, was prancing around, frequently lunging forward to shriek something unintelligible into a microphone. The drummer, thin enough to be a male anorexic, thrashed his head from side to side, apparently in the throes of musical ecstasy. If he'd asked me, I'd have advised the bass guitarist not to perform shirtless, as his bony, hollow-chested physique didn't add anything to the pelvic thrusts he was performing in time to the beat.

"Who are they?" I bellowed to Chantelle, indicating the band on the stage.

I thought she yelled back, "Rat's Piss," but I could have been mistaken.

I looked around. The room wasn't all that large, but it was crammed with people dancing. Around the sides other patrons perched at rickety tables and shouted conversations at each other. Built into one wall was a bar, crowded with individuals fighting each other to get to the front so they could catch the eye of the lone barman.

With an earsplitting crescendo, the band ended what had to be a song, although I hadn't recognized any melody to speak of or made out a single word. People clapped and called out approvingly, possibly because the racket had stopped. In the comparative quiet, I realized my ears were ringing. "Loud, aren't they?" I said to Chantelle.

"Makes up for talent," she said. "Look, there's Quip."

Quip glanced our way at the same time and beckoned eagerly for us to join him at his little table. We had to make our way around the perimeter, as the sound system had started blasting out a dancing beat, galvanizing those hanging around on the floor into frenzied action again.

I like dancing. Not the sort I learned at Madame Syke's Ballroom Dancing Academy when I was attending Wollegudgerie High. At that time my main claim to fame was how consistently I mashed my partner's toes. What I really liked was the fling-yourself-around type of dancing, where partners are optional. Although, when I thought of it, I'd had some awfully nice slow dances with Raylene...

Don't go there, I said to myself, feeling the dismals coming on. Fortunately the dance track drowned out my words.

When we finally got to Quip, he leapt up and gave each of us a hug. He really was the nicest bloke. I was sure I wasn't the first to wonder how he ever got himself married to Fran. Apart from the fact that he was clearly so totally gay, how someone with such a sunny nature could put up with Fran's bleak view of the world was a bit of a puzzle.

Quip wasn't his real name, though I wouldn't have been surprised if it had been. I'd come across some very strange monikers since I'd hit L.A.. Melodie had explained to me that Quip believed "Quip Trent" on the front page of a script promised more than "Bruce Trent." He could be right. I've never liked the name Bruce, although that may be because of my revolting cousin Brucie.

"Kylie! How's it going?" Quip asked, grabbing two chairs from a table next to us someone had momentarily deserted.

"Pretty good," I said. "I've got my first case."

Quip squeezed the chairs between the wall and the table, which I saw was fastened to the floor so it couldn't be moved. Chantelle and I managed to wriggle onto our seats, although everything was so crammed together, you had to practically breathe sideways to get any air.

"Where's Fran?" I asked, raising my voice to be heard above the din.

Quip pointed at the mass of people dancing. "In there, somewhere."

I caught sight of Fran almost immediately. "She's a ripper dancer, isn't she?" I said, astonished. Somehow the thought of Fran being expert in this area had never occurred to me. But then, why would it? She was anything but light-footed around the office.

"I can't keep up with her," said Quip, grinning as he watched Fran gyrate by us. "That gal was born to dance." He switched his attention to Chantelle and me. "What do you want to drink?"

Given the crush at the bar, I don't know how he did it, but a few minutes later Quip was back with beers for all of us, and one for Fran, when she eventually made it back to the table.

We clinked cans and glugged a mouthful or two. It felt good. Carrying on a shouted conversation had made me thirsty.

"Fran told me about your very first clients," Quip said to me. "Twins, aren't they? I don't remember their names."

"Alf and Chicka Hartnidge," announced Chantelle with the satisfied smile of one who has access to sources of information denied to many. I hadn't told her a thing yet about the Hartnidges, but I knew who had.

Chantelle confirmed her source by saying, "Melodie has a date with Chicka tonight. Can't wait to hear about it." I had a bet with myself the receptionist network would be humming tomorrow.

She hadn't finished. Leaning forward to speak confidentially, which was ridiculous, because everyone had to yell to be heard, Chantelle said, "Would you believe it? The Hartnidge brothers have Marty-O as their agent. And he's got Lamb White committed to a movie deal."

"Oh, God," said Quip, his handsome face showing deep disgust. "You know what doing business with Lamb White means, don't you? That creep Brother Owen and his off-the-planet Church of Possibilities will get involved. That sucks."

"Who's Marty-O? Who's Brother Owen, and what is the Church of Possibilities?" I asked.

Quip and Chantelle looked at each other, then switched their combined stares to me.

"*What*?" I said.

"You've never heard of Marty O. Ziema?"

"Not a sausage." From their expressions, they needed more. "I know nothing about him. Wouldn't know the bloke if I fell over him. Who is he?"

"Uber-agent," said Quip.

"Known throughout the biz as Marty-O," said Chantelle.

"Industry," said Quip.

Chantelle blinked at him.

"Those in the know," said Quip, "call it the industry, not the biz."

"Oh," said Chantelle. She seemed to be blushing. "I knew that."

CHAPTER SIX

Early the next morning, I was walking briskly home from Chantelle's apartment in West Hollywood. I'd planned this yesterday; I'd put a sports bag with shorts, a T-shirt, and running shoes in Chantelle's Jeep when she'd picked me up last night.

I'd discovered that even at the best of times, Chantelle was not what you'd call an early riser. Besides, this morning she'd be in a rush to get to her new job on time, so it was easier for me to get myself back to Kendall & Creeling. It wasn't that far, a couple of kilometers or so, but it was mostly uphill, so I was getting a good workout.

As I walked, I mused about Chantelle and me. Last night had been lovely. Chantelle was a warm and considerate lover, no strings attached, so at the moment I didn't have to worry where our relationship might go—I could just enjoy it.

So far we'd always ended up at her place, never mine. I used the excuse that her bed was king-size and so much more comfortable for two, but I knew that wasn't the real reason I never suggested we go back to my room at Kendall & Creeling.

That was it: Creeling.

Although technically I owned one percent more of the business than she did, in essence the building was home to Ariana Creeling's private eye company. Even when she wasn't there, Ariana was always present in some way, her personality palpable in her empty office. I just wouldn't be comfortable having Chantelle stay the night.

That got me wondering if I'd ever look at Ariana as just a person who happened to be my business partner. I couldn't imagine it would ever happen—not after that kiss.

How many different people had I kissed in my romantic career? Quite a few. Some of those kisses had been dynamite, some merely pleasant, some frankly yuck. I recalled sloppy kisses and cool kisses and swallow-your-tongue kisses and kisses that made my knees go weak...

And then there was Ariana.

One kiss, that's all we'd had, in a highly charged moment of danger. If I shut my eyes I could still feel her lips on mine, her arms around me. Not to be too fanciful, but that moment had been like being struck by lightning. *So this is what it is*, I remember thinking. *This is the person. This is the connection I've been looking for my whole life.*

Unfortunately, Ariana didn't share this earthshaking insight of mine. She'd backed off, apologized. A spur-of-the-moment kiss of little significance was the message. "I'm sure you'll agree," she'd said, quite kindly, "that close personal relationships in the workplace should be avoided. They just cause complications."

I'd almost blurted out, "Complications are what I want!" but I didn't. I played it cool, knowing instinctively that if I pushed it, Ariana would retreat to a place where I could never reach her. And I was determined to reach her, however long it took.

When I got to Kendall & Creeling, I checked the car park to see what vehicles were there. My rental, of course. And the battered pickup belonging to Luis the cleaner. No one else. Even Lonnie, who liked to get an early start, hadn't yet arrived.

I made a bit of a racket opening the front door and coming into the building. I'd threatened Luis with a golf club the first time we'd met, and he'd never forgotten it. Whenever I ran into him I couldn't help noticing he always kept a close eye on me and never let me get behind him.

"G'day, Luis," I said, meeting him on my way to the kitchen. He was a little bloke, who seemed a rather down-in-the-mouth type. I'd never heard him whistle or sing as he worked, though that might be because of me. For all I knew, Luis sang like a canary on his other cleaning jobs.

Right now he was holding a wastepaper basket at chest height, like a shield. He nodded warily at my greeting but kept his lips tightly closed.

"I'm thinking of learning Spanish," I said with a big smile. "Maybe I can practice on you."

Luis took a step back.

* * *

Julia Roberts, irritated because I'd been out all night, joined me in the kitchen while I made myself a pot of tea—loose leaf Twinings Orange Pekoe—and a bowl of porridge.

"Sorry to have left you alone, Jules," I said, when even a food bribe failed to wipe the scowl from her furry face. It amazed me how she could achieve such an unmistakable expression with just a few subtle adjustments of ears and whiskers.

I headed for my office, leaving her glowering at the crab-and-shrimp-flavored treats I'd put in her dish. Maybe Jules was right. I didn't think I'd fancy that combination for breakfast.

Last night I'd got a fair amount of information out of Quip about Lamb White et cetera, and I wanted to jot it down before the details faded. I needed to be prepared for my next meeting with my clients—that word gave me a bit of a thrill—who were due in my office at eleven o'clock. I was hoping Melodie would be back from her audition for a tooth-whitening commercial well before then.

Lamb White Incorporated specialized in G-rated movies for family viewing. I knew the sort, syrupy goody-goody stories where people smile and cry a lot, but never, ever swear or have sex. The company was part of the business empire of Brother Owen, a wealthy televangelist, whose New Age Church of Possibilities had sucked lots of celebrities into its congregation. Quip described Brother Owen as an obscenely rich con artist who had ripped off millions from trusting individuals who freely gave money to support the bogus belief system he was peddling.

The movie company, Lamb White Incorporated, was run by a woman called Tami Eckholdt. Quip wasn't too keen on her either. He said she came over as warm and caring, but underneath she was a combination of Phyllis Schlafly and Anita Bryant, only worse. When he explained who these two were, I saw what he meant. "A poisonous sheila?" I'd said. He'd agreed that pretty well summed up Tami Eckholdt.

I took my *Complete Handbook* with me when I went to sit in for Melodie at the reception desk. I was well into the chapter "Liars and How to Spot Them" and wanted to get things straight in my head before Alf and Chicka turned up. If they were lying to me, I needed to know.

In fact, the more I thought about it, the more I realized reliable lie detection would be an asset for any private investigator. Achieving this, however, was harder than I'd imagined. My handbook confidently stated that lies were detected only slightly more than half the time, which wasn't much better than just guessing. And worse, the better you knew someone, the less likely you were to know they were lying to you, because your feelings got in the way, plus the person had learned how to fool you.

I stopped reading to ponder whether Ariana had ever lied to me.

"Good morning, Kylie." Harriet Porter's smile lit up her face. "You studying something?"

Harriet had a voice like smoky honey, thick chestnut hair, and a top personality. She juggled law classes with part-time work for Kendall & Creeling. Add to that the fact she was pregnant, though not showing much yet, and you had someone who had an awful lot going on in her life. Me, I'd have been flat out just keeping up, but Harriet seemed to sail on through, like nothing really got to her. Maybe it had something to do with the fact that she was in a great relationship with Beth, or maybe Harriet was just one of those fortunate people who can cope, no matter what.

"I'm reading up on lying," I said. "Did you know that a person's blink rate can be a dead giveaway?"

"I think I heard that somewhere."

"The normal rate of blinking is twenty times a minute," I informed her.

Harriet grinned. "That much? You'd think we'd all wear our eyelids out. Or they'd become muscle-bound."

I had to laugh at that. Harriet had a bonzer sense of humor. "And Harriet, if people blink much faster, like up to a hundred times a minute, they're under pressure and probably lying."

"Maybe the person has something in their eye," Harriet suggested. She wasn't taking this at all seriously.

The front door banged behind Fran. She gave us both a gimlet stare. "Morning," she snarled.

If Quip could manage to be cheerful while married to Fran, the least I could do was be positive. "Last night was super, wasn't it?" I said with a jolly smile.

"You had a girls' night out?" inquired Harriet.

"When hell freezes over," muttered Fran.

I reminded myself that both these people belonged to my staff. In the interests of a good office atmosphere, I decided a little social chitchat would be in order. "Chantelle tells me Quip used to be a life coach," I said to Fran.

"Quip used to be lots of things." Fran's tone didn't invite further conversation, but I soldiered on.

"Did Quip ever life-coach you?"

Harriet chuckled. Fran gave me a long look, then said, "What the hell do you mean?"

"I was wondering if Quip was your life coach somewhere along the line."

"Why would I need a life coach?"

"Well, it'd be free, for one thing. And Quip could help you identify and meet your goals."

Fran said to Harriet, "Is she for real?"

Harriet chuckled again. Fran swung her gaze back to me. "For your information, Kylie, if it's any of your business—which it isn't—Quip gave up his life-coaching career long before I met him. If he'd still been doing it, I would have demanded he stop, because—" She broke off to glare at me suspiciously. "What are you looking at?"

I didn't want to own up, but Fran, hands on hips, was waiting for an answer. "How often you blink. It's research."

Fran rolled her eyes. "How often I blink? Jesus!"

"The rate you blink can be a giveaway if you're lying."

Fran's eyes narrowed down to slits. "You're accusing me of lying?" she ground out.

"Crikey, not in a million years," I said. "I'm not that brave."

* * *

Melodie breezed in at about quarter past ten. "They loved my laugh," she said, dumping assorted bags on the reception desk. Melodie had confided in me that she always traveled with masses of makeup and several outfits, just in case she needed to transform herself for a particular audition.

She gave a practiced toss of her long blond hair, then flashed her pearly whites at me. "Larry, my agent, thinks I'm a sure thing." Melodie looked at the ceiling, as if a choir of harmonizing angels might burst through, all singing "Sure thing! Sure thing!"

"You've got a callback already?" I was learning the lingo fast.

"Of course not. They've still got piles of bees to audition."

Bees was the term Melodie used for would-be actors. I reckoned it applied to Melodie, too, but thought it wiser not to say so.

"It's my big chance, Kylie. I just know it. You have to follow your dream."

"Your dream is to be in a tooth-whitening commercial?"

I must have sounded a touch sarcastic, because Melodie's expression changed from joyful to severe. "Refulgent is the nation's largest-selling dental enhancer."

"The largest? Blimey, that makes all the difference."

Melodie looked at me suspiciously—a lot of people had been doing that lately—but my innocent expression saved me. "Larry, my agent, says my laugh clinched it."

I put up a hand. "Don't demonstrate. I couldn't stand to hear it one more time." Curiosity made me add, "How does the laugh fit in with a tooth whitener anyway?"

"You must have heard the Refulgent jingle, 'Laugh Without Fear.' "

"Sorry. Don't know it."

Melodie patted my shoulder consolingly. "It's understandable. You *are* a complete stranger, after all?"

"I'm learning as fast as I can," I said in protest.

But Melodie had forgotten my cultural plight and was obviously reliving her moment of triumph at the audition. Clasping her hands, she exclaimed with deep emotion, "Refulgent! Now I can laugh without fear." She tinkled the infuriating laugh we'd all learnt to cringe at, then stretched her lips in a manic smile. "Thank you, Refulgent! Thank you!"

"That's it?" I said.

Melodie whirled on me like a demented creature. "It's a *speaking* part, Kylie. Do you know how hard it is to get one of those? Do you have any idea?" She took a deep breath to calm herself. "Anyone can look good, but to have words to interpret takes one to an entirely different level in the performing arts."

The phone rang. "All yours," I said, relinquishing the chair behind the reception desk. "Here's the list of calls and messages I've taken." Apparently, Melodie wasn't going to thank me for spending all this time covering for her, so I added sarcastically, "And thank you, Kylie, from the bottom of my heart."

Melodie didn't hear me. "Tiffany!" she shrieked into the phone. "This audition's the one. I feel it here." She thumped her chest. "What? Chicka? Yes, we went out last night…" Melodie slid a sideways look at me. "Tiff? I'll call you back…"

* * *

Ariana joined me in my office fifteen minutes before Alf and Chicka were due to arrive. "Bob just called me. There's a fender bender on the Hollywood Freeway and he's stuck in traffic, so he's going to be late for the Hartnidge meeting. Do you mind if I sit in?"

"Bonzer idea." I came around her side of the desk. Ariana was a little shorter than me, but we were pretty close to eye-to-eye. I wondered if she knew what an electric jolt it was to look into that startling blue. Then, of course, I realized she had to know. I reckoned from the time she was little, people had remarked on the color of her eyes.

Ariana raised an eyebrow. "Kylie?"

I felt my face get hot. I'd been staring. "I've been strategizing," I said hastily, gesturing to chairs I'd arranged around a coffee table I'd lugged in from Lonnie's office, where it had been buried under piles of papers and odd electronic devices. "I reckon if I sit Alf and Chicka over there, not together, but separate, and offer tea and biscuits, it'll create the kind of atmosphere where they'll be at ease."

I never found out what Ariana thought of this, because there was a knock at the door and Alf and Chicka sailed in. Their clothes were identical to yesterday, except each wore a pair of khaki pants instead of shorts.

"Told Melodie we could find our own way," said Chicka.

"Sorry we're a bit early," said Alf. "Chicka and me, we had a breakfast meeting with Tami, and we finished sooner than expected."

"That'd be Tami Eckholdt of Lamb White Incorporated?" I said in a casual, I'm-on-top-of-it way.

"Yeah, that Tami," said Chicka. "Friendly sort, and a bit of all right, I can tell you."

Being influenced by Quip's assessment of Tami Eckholdt, I hadn't considered for a moment she'd be sexually attractive. I now recalled *The Complete Handbook* counseled against accepting other people's opinions about individuals. A private investigator had to form his or her own judgments after rigorous examination of the person in question.

"Would you like to sit over here?" I said, ushering them in the direction of the coffee table assemblage.

"Right you are," said Alf. He and his twin brother flung themselves into chairs side by side. This was not the configuration I intended, but I could hardly ask them to move.

Alf winked at Ariana as he patted the nearest empty seat. "Park yourself here." When she complied, he asked, "How's tricks?"

"Tricks are fine, Mr. Hartnidge."

"Call me Alf? I reckon Mr. Hartnidge would be our dad, and he fell off the perch years ago."

"Tea and biscuits?" I said.

Alf shook his head. "Thanks, love, but no. Tami put on quite a spread for us." He jerked his head at his brother. "Chicka's got all the stuff you asked for about the staff and whatnot." Chicka obligingly whipped out copies of personnel files and handed them to me.

"How did you choose your staff?" I asked.

Alf pursed his lips. "Let's see. We wanted to bring our own people over, but immigration's hell these days, so it turned out to be more trouble than it was worth."

"That's when Tami stepped in," said Chicka. "Loaned us some Lamb White people and helped us hire a few others. Couldn't have set up the office without her."

I thought the rest of the meeting went quite well. I had a list of points to cover, and we went through all of them without too much trouble. The Hartnidges had had an investigator looking into the Australian end, but Alf and Chicka were convinced someone in their newly set up Burbank offices was the mastermind behind the opal scam.

"Not that Tami would know anything about it," said Chicka gallantly.

"We've got several Oz Mob shipments still on the way," said Alf. "God knows how many have opals in them."

"Vital Tami never hears a word about our little problem," Chicka cautioned. "If even a hint of anything illegal gets out, there goes the whole shebang."

Alf nodded sagely. "Moral clause in our Lamb White contract. No scandal. Nothing illegal." He jabbed Ariana with his elbow. "Takes all the fun out of life, eh?"

She looked at him for a sec, as if she couldn't believe he'd whacked her in the ribs. "I can see it could be a real downer," she said.

"So that's the sitch." Alf leaned back in his chair. "We'll leave it up to you experts to decide the next step."

The brothers turned to me, clearly expecting I'd know what this next step might be. "We'll do a comprehensive check on members of staff at your Burbank offices, then get back to you," I said.

Alf slapped his hands on his thighs. "Well, that's business taken care of. Now to pleasure." He beamed at Ariana. "Hope you don't mind me being a bit pushy, love, but are you free?"

Ariana looked startled for a moment, then said, "Pardon me?"

"I'd reckon a good sort like you would've been snapped up, but Melodie told Chicka, no, she'll be open to an invite. That's dinkum, isn't it? You're not hitched?"

I glanced at Ariana. She had an expression of polite inquiry. "I'm not sure what you mean, Mr. Hartnidge."

"Alf," said Alf.

"He's asking you out," said Chicka helpfully.

Alf nodded vigorously. "Yeah. A slap-up meal, a show, whatever takes your fancy."

Silence. Both Alf and Chicka gazed at Ariana.

"Could be the best offer you get all week," I remarked.

The corners of Ariana's mouth twitched. "I'm honored, Alf," she said, "but I'm afraid it's a rule of the company never to date clients."

Clearly disappointed, he said, "A rule, eh? A strict one?"

"Very strict. But thank you so much for asking."

I saw them out, then came back to my office. Ariana was still there. We grinned at each other.

"You missed your chance with Alf," I said severely. "He may not ask you again."

Ariana laughed. "I'll just have to be brave about it."

CHAPTER SEVEN

As soon as Bob came in, shaking his head over freeway traffic—"It's a nightmare, and it's getting worse"—I filled him in on the meeting Ariana and I had had with Alf and Chicka. Unable to resist, I also told him how Alf had asked Ariana out on a date.

Bob's narrow face was split with a wide grin. "And I had to be stuck in traffic. You have all the fun, Kylie."

We discussed Lamb White and the Church of Possibilities, which Bob said was usually shortened to COP. "Calling a church COP doesn't sound very religious," I said.

With a cynical laugh, Bob said, "COP isn't a religion. It's a money-making machine for Brother Owen. And he's a total fake too."

"So why do all these people support him?"

Bob shook his head. "He's one of the great televangelist con men. Wait until you see him in action."

I went off to find Lonnie and give him the Oz Mob staff list for the Burbank offices. Lonnie's room was an indescribable mess, but he always seemed to be able to find what he was searching for in the piles of electronic devices, folders, binders, loose papers, and the like. He was hunched over a monitor, sitting in the only chair in the room that didn't have gear on it. He was operating the keyboard with one hand while stuffing a doughnut into his mouth with the other. Maybe I was influenced by the doughnut, but I thought he looked even plumper than usual this morning.

"You weren't here earlier," I said, "so I couldn't ask before I borrowed a coffee table." I pointed to the crowded corner where I'd found it. "The table looks pretty good in my office, so I was wondering if you wanted it back. I thought I could replace it with a cabinet, or shelving, or something like that. Be more useful, wouldn't it?"

With a practiced move, Lonnie shoved back the lock of brown hair that habitually fell over one eye, giving him a Peter Pan boyish look. "You can have the table, but what did you do with the stuff that was on it?"

"I put everything neatly on the floor." I didn't add it was the only neat area in the whole place.

Lonnie peered in the direction I'd indicated. "Oh, yeah, I see it." He gave me a stern look. "It may seem a trifle disorganized in here, Kylie, but I have a mental grid system and know exactly where everything is. That's why it's important that nobody move anything."

"Does Luis come in here?"

"The cleaner?" Lonnie was obviously horrified. "He's forbidden to enter this room. And don't you ever, out of some psychotic desire for order, encourage him to!"

"No worries. Luis and I aren't what you'd call close."

Lonnie jerked his head at the papers I held in my hand. "Something for me?"

"Background checks. High priority." I couldn't help adding, "My first dinky-di case, actually."

Grinning he said, "A dinky-di case, is it? What's that, some peculiar Aussie sexual practice?" He gave me a pretend leer. "Want to try it on me, little girl?" he asked, twirling an imaginary mustache.

"You're out of luck," I said. "Dinky-di means true, genuine. Like it's my first real case."

He took the Oz Mob staff records and glanced at them. "They've all got social security numbers. Piece of cake."

"That makes it easier?"

"Honey," said Lonnie dramatically, "give me your social security number and I can find out everything, and I mean everything, about you."

"I've got nothing to hide."

"Everyone's got something to hide." He rustled the pages. "What am I looking for here?"

I gave him a quick rundown on the smuggled opal situation, and how the Hartnidges couldn't report the crime because it would derail their movie with Lamb White.

"I ran into Melodie in the kitchen," said Lonnie, "and she couldn't wait to tell me all about her date last night with Chicka Hartnidge."

"More than she told *me*."

"Ah, but you're management, sweetheart."

I grinned at him, rather pleased. "I suppose I am."

"Chicka took her to a British pub down in Santa Monica. Packed to the rafters with Brits. Melodie said she sang rugby songs, tried a lot of different beers, and played darts."

I found this difficult to visualize, though what did I know of the intimate details of Melodie's social life? It was unlikely, but for all I knew, singing rugby songs, drinking beer, and playing darts was second nature to her.

Lonnie went on, "Melodie says Chicka's promised she can voice one of the characters in the puppet movie he and his brother are making with Lamb White."

I was aghast. "You're kidding me!"

Amused, Lonnie said, "I kid you not."

"But all the characters in the movie are Australian animals. They'll speak with Aussie accents."

"I pointed that out, but Melodie declared if Meryl could do an Aussie accent, so could she." He sent me one of his charming, dimpled smiles. "In fact, I believe Melodie's going to ask you to coach her. After all, you speak Aussie quite fluently, don't you?"

* * *

I headed for reception. I was going to front up to Melodie and tell her she had a snowball's chance in hell of having me coach her in Aussie. But she wasn't there. Harriet was sitting behind the desk. This was too much.

"Melodie's off on an audition again?" There was an edge in my voice.

Harriet's expression was grave. "I'd say she wished she was. Ariana's got Melodie in her office, and she's reading her the riot act."

"Oh." Ariana had come in while I was still covering reception this morning, and, although all she'd said to me was "Good morning," her expression had made it clear she wasn't pleased to find Melodie absent and me there.

"Oh, indeed." said Harriet. "You haven't seen Ariana on the warpath, Kylie. I have. Believe me, it's scary."

I reckoned I didn't need to ask what Ariana was on the warpath about, but I did wonder why it had taken her so long to get jack of Melodie's constant absences.

My expression must have given me away. Harriet said, "Why's it taken Ariana so long? You couldn't know, but there's some history between them."

My imagination leapt around wildly. Was Melodie Ariana's love child? She'd have had to be a child herself when she had Melodie if that were the case…

"Ariana knew Melodie's mother," said Harriet, canceling out that particularly alarming scenario. "I'm sure you know that Ariana used to be an LAPD cop. She served with Sharon Schultz at the same station, and they became very close friends."

How close? My imagination got ready to jump again.

Oblivious to this, Harriet went on, "Sharon was a single mother, totally estranged from her ex-husband, and with no family of her own. When she was diagnosed with advanced breast cancer, she begged Ariana to keep an eye on Melodie, should the worst happen."

"And the worst happened?"

"Eventually, after a long, bitter battle against the cancer. Melodie was in her mid teens when her mother died. Fortunately, her father entered the picture again, not that he was much use, but better than nothing. He encouraged Melodie to go for a career in show business, but as you know, that rarely pays the bills, so a couple of years ago Melodie approached Ariana and begged her for a job to tide her over until she made the big time. The agreement was that Melodie could go to auditions, but she had to schedule them at lunchtime or after work."

I had many questions but no chance to ask them, because at that moment Melodie appeared, her face anguished. "My career may be over," she announced. She didn't actually put the back of one hand to her forehead in the proper tragic fashion, but heartbreak was in every drooping line of her body.

"You won't be a receptionist anymore?"

Melodie broke out of her misery to give me an irate glare. "My *acting* career, Kylie."

Harriet grinned. I said, "My mistake."

"Besides," said Melodie, "being a receptionist isn't what I'd call a career. It's more a filler. Something you do until you're discovered."

"What happens if you're never discovered?" I inquired.

Irritated, Melodie clicked her tongue. "It's the bees who are never discovered. I'm not a bee."

The phone rang. Harriet gestured to Melodie to take the call. Glowering at this unwarranted interruption, Melodie snatched it up. She really could act. Her voice full of warm interest, she said, "Good morning, Kendall & Creeling. How may I be of help to you?"

Harriet and I had turned away, when we were jolted by a shriek from Melodie. "Larry! Larry! Awesome!"

Melodie, the receiver pressed to her bosom, gazed at us wide-eyed. "Larry, my agent, says I have a callback tomorrow! He says they've told him I'm practically a sure thing! I'm going to be a Refulgent girl!"

To make sure we got the picture, Melodie tinkled her Refulgent laugh.

"Will I kill her, or will you?" Harriet asked.

* * *

Hand raised to knock, I stood outside Ariana's brass-studded door. I felt a touch of trepidation, even though I'd rehearsed what I was going to say. I'd remain calm and speak with measured, cool tones, as I reminded Ariana that she and I were co-owners of Kendall & Creeling. That being so, any discipline of staff—in this case, Melodie—should have involved me too.

Ariana would be likely to point out that it was me who had made it easy for Melodie to skip off to the audition, because I volunteered to answer the phone for her. Better to bring this up myself, before Ariana did.

Also, I'd had a bright idea for the Hartnidge case and wanted to run it by her. I was expecting some opposition, which was understandable. Last time I had a lash at an undercover role, I'd got a black eye for my trouble, but this time would be different. I'd be super cautious. Besides, I was more experienced now.

Thinking about that, I decided not to mention experience. I had made a bit of a hash of things in the past, and but for Julia Roberts, might not be around at all.

I took a deep breath, knocked sharply, then opened the door. "It's me."

"So I see," said Ariana, looking faintly amused. "Come on in."

I came in and sat down. Ariana leaned back in her black chair behind her black desk. As usual, she herself was wearing black. I had the sudden thought that maybe Ariana was in long-term mourning for Melodie's mother, Sharon Schultz. Though if that were so, it would be years...But then, Queen Victoria wore widow's black for the rest of her long life, after Prince Albert died.

"Kylie?"

I became aware that Ariana was waiting for me to speak. In a rush, I blurted out, "Melodie's got a callback for the Refulgent commercial."

"She's had plenty of those before."

"Ah, but this time Larry-my-agent says she's a sure thing."

A crease appeared between Ariana's elegant eyebrows. "Larry is your agent?"

"No, he's not, of course. But haven't you noticed how Melodie always calls him Larry-my-agent, like it's one word? It's sort of sticks in my mind that way."

I was making a complete galah of myself. I hadn't kept to my plan, and this was the sorry result. I'd pretend this bit of the conversation hadn't happened, and start again.

"Ariana," I said, "I've got something important to discuss with you."

"Before you do, I want to apologize. I should have consulted you before I spoke with Melodie about the time she's spending at auditions when she should be here, doing her job. Seeing you sitting at the reception desk this morning, answering the phone, was the final straw."

Feeling a jab of guilt that Melodie was taking all the blame, I said, "It's not like Melodie made me do it. I volunteered."

"You're a partner in the company. Melodie had no right to presume on your good nature."

Half of me rejoiced that Ariana was speaking of me as her business partner. The other half was embarrassed at how pliable I'd been. "I should have been tougher. I'm just a pushover."

"No way are you a pushover, Kylie." Ariana's tone was dry, in fact, pretty close to sardonic. "Life would be much easier if you were." Before I could ask her what she meant, she went on, "You said you have something important to discuss with me?"

"I reckon I could go undercover at Alf and Chicka's business. Maybe I come in as a personal assistant, or an expert in PR, or something like that."

As I'd expected, Ariana looked skeptical. "And you'd be doing what?"

"Basically snooping around. No one would suspect me. Why would they? I'd just be an Aussie established in L.A., who'd be happy to pick up some work with an Australian company."

Ariana's phone rang. "Excuse me." She listened for a moment, then said to me, "Your Aunt Millie's calling from Wollegudgerie. Do you want to take it here?"

Considering the fact that I was about to make a strenuous effort to talk my aunt out of coming to L.A., I said, "I'd better take it in my office."

On the way down the hall, I marshaled all my arguments. It was to no avail. Aunt Millie's mind was set in concrete. "I'll arrive next Wednesday," she said. "And Kylie, I expect to see you waiting for me at the airport."

Wouldn't it rot your socks?

CHAPTER EIGHT

I was brooding at my desk, trying to work out how to keep Aunt Millie occupied so she didn't have a chance to interact too closely with anyone, when Harriet cheered me up by popping in to ask if Chantelle and I were free for dinner the next night.

"Maurice and Gary will be there," she said. "I'd love you to get to know them."

Maurice was Harriet's unborn child's dad, by way of a syringe. Gary was his long-term partner. I'd met them fleetingly one time they'd called in to collect Harriet when her car had died.

I told Harriet it was a yes for me, but I'd have to check with Chantelle. One advantage of having a relationship with a receptionist is that you can always get them on the phone, even if there are constant interruptions from calls or the necessity to exchange super-nice remarks with clients drifting by.

"Hold please," said Chantelle to me after I'd only got three words out. I heard her say warmly, "A very good afternoon to you, Mr. Duddle. It's wonderful weather we're having, isn't it?"

"Was that Frank Duddle, who directed *Afternoon of the Dancing Zombies*?" I asked when she got back to me.

"That's the one. He's a little guy, with a head as bald as a billiard ball. Hold on...Good afternoon, Ms. Sarandon. It's wonderful weather we're having, isn't it?"

"Why do you keep mentioning the weather?" I asked when Chantelle came back to me.

"Safe topic of conversation. And everyone's got a set of weather phrases to use."

"So let's say Tom Hanks waltzes in. I suppose you'd chat with him about the catastrophic effects of global warming?"

"Global warming's political." Chantelle's tone was severe. "A receptionist doesn't initiate discussion of politics or religion. And weather should never be controversial."

"Best to stick to 'It's not the heat, it's the humidity'?"

"You've got the idea," Chantelle said.

Having established she'd be delighted to dine at Harriet and Beth's place, I rang off. It was early Saturday morning at the 'Gudge—Aunt Millie had called at the crack of dawn there—so I had to wait at least an hour before calling Bluey Bates at home.

Bluey was Wollegudgerie's only lawyer, and he'd looked after all the stuff to do with my dad's will. His brother, Ralphie Bates, owned Ralphie's Opalarium, one of the jewelry stores making a good living selling opals to the tourists. A few months back, when I'd still been living at the Wombat's Retreat, the Opalarium had been burgled during a long weekend. Only the finest stones were taken, to a total value of a cool quarter of a million. The law in town, Sergeant Mucka Onslow, had been completely baffled. Not surprising, as most things baffled Mucka.

Maybe there was a connection between the Opalarium heist and the opals being smuggled into Los Angeles in the Kelvin Kookaburras. I wanted to sound Bluey out first, rather than his brother, because there'd been a pretty strong rumor that Ralphie had staged the whole thing to collect the insurance money.

I filled in the time before I could decently disturb Bluey Bates with Internet searches to turn up what I could on Brother

Owen, the Church of Possibilities, and Lamb White. Google threw up countless responses on each one.

Naturally, the Church of Possibilities had its own Web page. And what a Web page it was! As soon as I clicked on, a notice appeared saying that any necessary software to view the COP Web site would be automatically loaded, if necessary. I already had video capability, so after a short pause, a chorus of cherubim and seraphim, wings wildly flapping, burst into song, while below them Brother Owen, one hand raised in blessing, stood smiling beneficently. He wore flowing white robes with a bright blue sash.

I knew it was Brother Owen because the cherubim and seraphim were chanting "Bro-ther O-wen" rather like a crowd might at a football match.

Another click brought me a close-up of Brother Owen's welcoming face. He seemed in his forties and was handsome in a well-fed, self-satisfied way. "Has anyone, ever, really understood you? The real vibrant you?" he inquired in a deep, warm voice.

After a pause for his audience to consider the question, he went on, "Have you been allowed to express fully the breathtaking talents that lie within you?"

Another pause. "Ask yourself, deep in your heart, are you really appreciated by those around you? Appreciated as your unique, astonishing self *should* be appreciated?"

Brother Owen allowed himself a small, sympathetic smile. "Do you wonder, in the dark hours before dawn, *Is this all there is?*"

Really long pause, then, "I am here to tell you there is more! More!"

The screen changed to a longer shot. Brother Owen's arms were extended as if he were about to step forward and embrace the viewer. "I am a harbinger of glory! I have been sent with wonderful tidings of great joy to all who will listen. Come to the Church of Possibilities! Discover the brilliant future that is your birthright! Cast off the shackles that have held you back, and rise to the heights you truly deserve!"

After this overload of Brother Owen, it was a relief to go to my e-mail. I deleted spam, answered messages from my friends back in Oz, and read the PI newsletter to which I'd recently subscribed, which had a fascinating but rather yucky article on bodily fluids. By then it was time to ring Bluey Bates.

"Kylie, mate! How the bloody hell are you?"

I could picture Bluey's freckled face and ginger hair. In the perverse Aussie way, redheads were often called Blue or Bluey. "Not bad, not bad at all," I said.

"Keeping the Yanks on their toes, are you?"

"More like they're keeping me on mine."

"So what can I do you for, mate?"

"This is confidential, Bluey."

"Lips sealed, Kylie, old love. Lips sealed."

"Has anything come of the investigation into the robbery at Ralphie's Opalarium?"

"Not a thing." Bluey's voice had hardened. He and Ralphie didn't see eye-to-eye over most subjects. "My brother's a lucky bastard, Kylie. The insurance company's going to pay up."

"You don't think they should?"

Bluey's snort came clearly over the line. "Let's put it this way, I reckon Ralphie's fairy godmother had to bust a gut to keep him out of the hands of the boys in blue."

"You believe Ralphie had something to do with the burglary?"

"Too right, I do, but I haven't said a word about it to Mucka. I'm not about to dob in my own brother." He snorted again. "Pity I've got gold-plated scruples, eh, Kylie?"

We discussed the burglary for a bit, then I asked Bluey if he knew the Hartnidge brothers. "Top blokes, both of 'em," he declared. "Done a bit of legal work for their Oz Mob company. Alf and Chicka pay on time and in full. You can't ask for much more than that."

"You certainly can't." I knew Bluey was struggling to carve out a decent living in Wollegudgerie, which had to make him even madder about his brother's possible insurance rip-off.

Bluey paused, then said, "I'm getting the strong feeling you're seeing some sort of connection between Ralphie's missing opals and the Hartnidge twins. Would I be right?"

I trusted Bluey implicitly. He'd handled legal work for Mum's pub, and he'd looked after me and my inheritance. He had a rep for being as honest as the day is long. I told him everything I knew.

Bluey whistled. "So that's the explanation for the city bloke who's been sniffing around. He's a private investigator. You can tell the Hartnidges he's not much chop. He won't get much out of anyone here in the 'Gudge. No one likes a nosy parker."

Bluey went on to give me the latest gossip, including my cousin Brucie's claim that I was begging him to join Kendall & Creeling. I set Bluey straight on that. We said goodbye, with Bluey promising to call me if he heard anything interesting to do with the stolen opals.

I'd scribbled notes as we'd talked, so I typed them up and put them in the new folder I'd started, titled HARTNIDGE, ALF & CHICKA.

I grinned to myself as I put the folder in my near-empty filing cabinet. Crikey, for a moment there I'd felt like a real PI!

* * *

It had become very clear to me that I had to prepare everyone at Kendall & Creeling for Aunt Millie's arrival. It just wouldn't be fair to have them caught unawares. First, my partner in the business had to be advised that someone was coming to town who'd give Fran a run for her money, and then some. Hell, she'd do Fran like a dinner.

Ariana was putting papers in her briefcase, ready to leave for the weekend. I knew she lived alone, apart from her gorgeous German shepherd, Gussie. I'd visited her house in the Hollywood Hills once, accompanied by Bob Verritt. It had been strictly business, worse luck.

The house was like her—elegant and self-contained. It had a fabulous view over Los Angeles. Maybe she often sat there with someone, admiring the city lights. Did she ever have dinner parties, like Harriet and Beth? Could Ariana even cook? There were so many things I didn't know about her—for example, the significance of the heavy gold signet ring she always wore.

"Got a mo?" I said. "My Aunt Millie from Wollegudgerie is lobbing in on Wednesday."

Ariana raised an eyebrow. It was a talent I didn't have but envied madly. "Have you always been able to raise one eyebrow, or did you have to practice?" I asked.

That got Ariana's other eyebrow into play. Then she laughed and shook her head.

"What?" I said.

"I dimly remember practicing as a kid," she answered, still smiling. "I thought it was an incredibly sophisticated thing to do."

That gave me a little thrill. Ariana was sharing something about her life with me. But I couldn't dwell on that; I had to give her an Aunt Millie alert.

"My aunt's flying in on Qantas."

"You've already said she's coming to town."

I knew I was stalling, so I made myself take the plunge. "Fact is, Ariana, she's what you'd call a bit of a character."

"Seems to run in the family," Ariana remarked.

"I didn't mean a *good* character."

"Your aunt's a criminal?" Ariana was grinning.

"No, but she has a very direct manner."

"An excellent quality."

"Don't laugh at me. This is serious."

Ariana's smile disappeared. "What's worrying you about your aunt's visit?"

"Aunt Millie prides herself on speaking her mind, and since she's dead-set down on most things, that means she's usually upsetting someone."

"You means she's a pessimist?"

"I mean nothing ever seems to please her."

Ariana chuckled. "I can hardly wait to see Millie and Fran meet up."

"I'm hoping to keep them apart."

Ariana looked at me thoughtfully. "This is a vacation for your aunt, is it?"

I debated whether to tell her the real reason behind Aunt Millie's trip. Maybe secretly Ariana still wanted to get rid of me and would be delighted to learn a family member was on the way to persuade me to come home.

My mum always says honesty is the best policy—she's big on clichés—so I said, "Mum wants me back at the Wombat's Retreat. Says she needs me to help run the pub. She and Aunt Millie have been talking."

"You mean your aunt's visit is to convince you to return to Australia?"

"Something like that."

Ariana didn't appear to be chuffed with this news. Actually, she was frowning. "What are your thoughts on this, Kylie?"

"I'm thinking Aunt Millie's trip is going to be a failure. And she won't be pleased."

"Well, that's her problem, isn't it?" Ariana picked up her briefcase. "Enjoy your weekend, and try not to worry about pesky relatives."

"I'll try," I said, without much hope I'd succeed.

* * *

I found Fran, Harriet, and Melodie in the kitchen. As I entered, Melodie was saying, "Chicka's real nice, but he didn't even try to get to first base. He's shy, you know. So sweet!"

"I'd call it boring," said Fran.

"Sounds refreshing to me?" said Harriet.

"Chicka's *not* boring," declared Melodie emphatically, tossing her hair around. I'd always admired how she could do that without getting a mouthful. "He's a *producer.*"

Fran glowered. "Any fool can call themselves a producer. Quip meets with phonies calling themselves producers all the time."

Melodie put her hands on her hips and glowered right back at Fran. "Chicka Hartnidge is *not* a phony. He's practically guaranteed I can voice one of the puppets in his Oz Mob movie."

"Really?" said Harriet, who unaccountably had missed out on this momentous news. "Which one?"

"Chicka hasn't actually said yet."

"A puppet's voice?" said Fran, lifting one side of her rosebud mouth. Great sneerer, Fran. "Won't you be overextending your artistic range, Melodie?"

There could be violence any minute, so I stepped in. "News flash, everyone. My Aunt Millie's coming to town next Wednesday. She's inclined to be critical and have a dark view of life. I'm telling you this so you won't take offense if she says something derogatory."

"I for one," said Fran, "*will* take offense. I loathe negativity."

I couldn't help a hoot of laughter. Knowing I'd regret it, I cheerfully gave into temptation. "Fran, old matey," I said, "you've single-handedly made negativity an art form."

Glower meltdown!

CHAPTER NINE

On Saturday morning a phone call from Bob Verritt interrupted my reading of the *L.A. Times*. Ariana had just called him about my suggestion of going undercover into the Hartnidges' Oz Mob operation in Burbank.

"My view is, it could work out well," Bob said. "Having someone on the inside could be a real advantage, if Alf and Chicka agree."

"Ariana isn't too keen on the idea, is she?"

"I'm afraid not. She brought up the beating your face took last time you went undercover."

Really indignant that Ariana clearly didn't believe I was capable of learning from my mistakes, I said, "If she thinks I'm going to cower in the corner, she's got another thing coming."

Bob chortled. "She's convinced you'll do quite the opposite to cowering. That's the problem."

"But she's not going to try and stop me?"

This seemed to amuse Bob even more. "Ariana doesn't fight battles she knows she'll lose."

Well, blow me down! It gave me a tingle of pleasure to think that just for once I had one up on Ariana.

We discussed the ins and outs of the undercover role I might play, then Bob rang off, saying he'd try to get hold of Alf and Chicka to sound them out about the idea.

My Saturday routine was to do laundry before I went out to stock up on provisions. Usually I took a moment to admire the washer and dryer setup I'd had installed, but this morning there were other things on my mind. I threw clothes into the washer with unnecessary force. It really irked me that Ariana didn't trust me not to be reckless.

This case was so important to me. For one thing, it had opals involved. And Aussies. I felt a momentary sisterhood with Melodie and her One Big Chance. This was my OBC. I could prove I had the makings of a private investigator if I brought the Hartnidge case to a successful conclusion.

I said to Julia Roberts, who I'd found sleeping on the dryer, "I've a good mind to give Ariana an earful. What do you say, Jules? Should I?"

Julia Roberts uncurled herself, stretched, then sat down, looking thoughtful. She blinked at me, once. I took this to mean yes. Before I could change my mind, I went back to my room, picked up the phone, and punched in Ariana's number, which I knew by heart, not that I'd ever needed to use it much.

She answered on the second ring with a cool "Hello."

"It's Kylie."

"Is something wrong?"

"No. Well, yes."

There was a pause. I was cursing myself. I should have worked out exactly what to say, before going off half-cocked.

Ariana said, "Are you going to tell me what it is?"

"Bob's just rung. You think I'm reckless, don't you?"

"Impetuous, perhaps."

"I'd prefer spontaneous," I snapped.

"How about impulsive?" Ariana laughed. "Shall I fetch the thesaurus? We can have dueling words at ten paces."

I had to smile. "I'm being a galah, aren't I?"

"I'm not quite sure what that is."

"It's a pink and gray cockatoo. Not the brightest bird on the branch. Essentially, I'm saying I'm a dumb cluck."

"You're not dumb. And perhaps you should be annoyed. I'm not treating you like my business partner. We should discuss all these issues and come to joint decisions."

Stone the crows! Two concessions from Ariana in twenty-four hours?

"Maybe you're right," I said. "I have to admit all I know about being a private eye could be written on the head of a pin in large letters."

She didn't rush to contradict me.

"So," I went on, "I promise to run things past either you or Bob before I do anything rash, hasty, hotheaded, foolhardy, spur-of-the-moment, devil-may-care, or precipitous."

I was grinning to myself, thinking how being first in my English class at school was paying off years later, when Ariana said, "I concede. You win. Duel over."

* * *

My day was all mapped out. After the laundry was in the dryer, I sallied forth to the nearest big supermarket. It had taken me a while, but I was getting used to the different brand names and the way Americans referred to biscuits as cookies, soft drinks as sodas, and lollies as candy.

I'd got a bit carried away shopping, so, laden with many bags, I had to make several trips from my car across the courtyard and in the front door. I kept a wary eye out for intruders. It'd been drummed into me that L.A. could be a dangerous city and that at any given moment violent crime was happening all over the place.

Julia Roberts helped me unpack things. Like all cats, she quite lost her dignity over bags and boxes, and leapt in and out of them like a kitten.

I had a wholesome avocado salad for lunch—rather spoiling the health side with lashings of mayonnaise—then I gave Julia

Roberts a good grooming. Since I'd adopted her, I'd made several trips to pet stores in search of suitably upmarket combs, brushes, and clippers. Only the best for Jules. She hated her feet being touched, so she objected strongly to the clippers, but that was too bad, as being mostly an inside cat she didn't wear her claws down.

Julia Roberts pretended she didn't like being fussed over, but it was a lie. She loved it. It probably helped that I assured her she was beautiful as I brushed her. On this point we were in complete agreement.

Then I heard a sound. Julia Roberts immediately went on wide-eyed alert. Had someone broken in? I looked around for a weapon. I'd kept the golf club with which I'd menaced Luis a few weeks ago, so I grabbed that.

"Kylie? It's me, Lonnie," a voice called out.

I put the golf club down. Lonnie would laugh if he saw me with it. Followed by Jules, I trotted out into the hall. Lonnie grinned at me. "Just catching up on some work. For you, actually—the backgrounds for the Oz Mob people you wanted."

He was in ancient jeans and a once-white T-shirt. His stomach bulged over the waistband. One of the reasons for this was in his hand: a bag bearing the McDonald's golden arches. Lonnie was notorious for being a fast-food junkie.

"Want some fries?" he said.

"No, thank you. No chips for me." We had McDonald's in Australia, complete with golden arches, but no way would they ever persuade me to call chips french fries.

It was funny how the atmosphere was different when someone other than just me was there. Knowing Lonnie was down the hall in his messy office changed the atmosphere subtly. And during the working week, it was different again. I wondered if energy fields around people charged the air in some way.

Mid afternoon, I went to ask Lonnie if he wanted a cup of tea. Julia Roberts had long deserted me, and I found her exploring Lonnie's cluttered room.

"Can you get that cat out of here?" he demanded, looking up from his computer screen. "I've asked her nicely, but she pays no attention."

"If you beg her to keep you company, she won't. Your mistake is to tell her to get lost."

Lonnie grunted. "I haven't got time to indulge in cat psychology."

"I've come to ask if you want a cuppa."

He was back peering at the screen. "Tea, you mean?"

"Yes, I've just made a pot."

"Hot?"

"Of course."

Lonnie looked at me over his shoulder. "I'd prefer iced tea. There's some in the fridge."

I shuddered. "That stuff is yours?"

"What's wrong with it?"

"It's *flavored*!"

Lonnie nodded. "Passion fruit and mango. Delicious."

I was thinking how my mother always says there's no accounting for tastes, when Lonnie squinted at me. "You should chill out," he said. "You're getting way too emotional over tea."

"Thank you for your advice, Lonnie."

My heavily sarcastic tone passed him by. "That's OK," he said.

Definitely time to change the subject. "How's it going?" I said, indicating the folder holding the names of Oz Mob's American staff.

He rubbed his chin. "What do you know about Tami Eckholdt?" he asked.

"She runs Lamb White for the Church of Possibilities. She helped Alf and Chicka get staff for their office."

"Tami Eckholdt's got her sister working for the Hartnidges but under a false name." He tapped the screen. "Look here. She's using the correct social security number but calling herself Paula Slade instead of Patsy Eckholdt."

"Why would she do that?"

Lonnie grinned at me. "You're the detective, remember?"

I got Lonnie his revoltingly flavored iced tea and took my own proper tea back to my office. Soon I was deep in *Private Investigation: The Complete Handbook.* The chapter on lying had me fascinated. I was up to the section describing how unconscious body movements give liars away. I would have thought fidgeting and fiddling were signs someone wasn't being truthful, but it turned out to be quite the opposite. Good liars tend to make fewer gestures, because they know such actions could signal they're worried about being found out. They don't touch their hair, or scratch their heads, or rub their hands together. They repress these movements.

But most fascinating of all, liars still give themselves away with bodily cues. While they're busily controlling hands, arms, and faces, they forget about the lower part of their bodies. It's the legs and feet that betray them. Even small adjustments unconsciously made can indicate tension and guilt.

Now, Ariana didn't make a lot of gestures, but in her case I thought it was simply that she was that kind of person—controlled, cool, constrained.

I made a mental note at the next opportunity to check out her lower body, anyway. The thought made me smile. I could imagine Ariana's reaction, should she catch me at it. "What *are* you doing?" she'd say. She wouldn't roll her eyes, but it'd be a close thing.

I visualized her lower body. Flat stomach, taut legs…

"That way lies madness," I remarked to Jules, who'd just strolled in the door. She yawned.

* * *

I was really looking forward to going to Harriet and Beth's that evening. They rented a house in Van Nuys. It was in the valley, or "over the hill" as I was learning to say.

I'd embarrassed myself the first time I'd had a stab at pronouncing Van Nuys, but now I confidently said "Van Eyes" with the best of them. Actually, having never learnt Spanish, I was rather at a disadvantage with some of the street and place names in Los Angeles. I hadn't yet fully mastered Cahuenga or Tujunga, and people had been known to giggle when I had a try at Camarillo.

It was my turn to drive, so I'd closely studied my *Thomas Guide* during the afternoon, intending to impress Chantelle with my grasp of L.A.'s geography. I was fine on the Hollywood Freeway, but once we hit the surface streets, I got into a complete pickle.

"I'm a total no-hoper at this navigating thing," I said to Chantelle, after she'd set me straight and we were heading more or less in the correct direction. "No probs at home in the 'Gudge, but here...I shook my head.

"Just how many streets does your hometown have?" Chantelle asked.

I had to admit Wollegudgerie was pretty small.

"And how many streets do you think are in Los Angeles?"

"Couldn't even hazard a guess."

"I rest my case," said Chantelle. "I believe we take a left here."

Left turns were still a challenge for me, as I tended to head for the left side of the road instead of the right, but this time I accomplished the feat relatively smoothly—Chantelle only covered her eyes for a moment—and soon we were drawing up in front of Harriet and Beth's house.

It was a compact house, white stucco with a red tile roof and a great big oak tree in the front. Harriet opened the front door before we got to ring the bell. "Any trouble finding us?"

"None," said Chantelle. I had to love the woman.

Maurice and Gary were already established in the living room, drinks in hand. We all did the welcoming routine, then Harriet pointed us to the little bar in the corner and said to help ourselves. Even though I'd spent most of my life in a pub, I wasn't what you'd call a hardened drinker, so I poured myself a glass of white wine. Chantelle hit the vodka.

Beth, who was obviously the cook for the evening, came in from the kitchen to greet us. She was a tall, rangy woman who bubbled with laughter most of the time. I'd met her at the office on several occasions and never saw her less than cheery, even when she encountered Fran.

"Kylie! Chantelle! How wonderful to see you!"

I said it was bonzer to see her too but couldn't help wondering if Beth ever had a down day. Did she ever grump around the house? Did gloom ever slump her shoulders? Could she possibly always be this upbeat?

I had a vision of Harriet barking, "For God's sake, Beth, stop laughing and be serious!" But then, Harriet was a cheerful sort too. They were probably perfectly suited, which was fortunate, since they were to be parents in a few months.

Maurice was the sperm donor for the child Harriet was carrying, and I recalled her saying he was genetically superior. While everyone was chatting about how unbelievably expensive homes were in L.A., I picked up that Maurice was a real estate agent. I considered him closely. Would I buy a house from this man?

Maurice was very neat and reserved. I noticed he listened a lot more than he spoke. He looked as if he'd just that moment shaved and patted on some exclusive aftershave. Checking out his hands, I found his fingernails were manicured. He had short, dark hair and a hard, every-day-at-the-gym body, which he showed off with a very tight red T-shirt and snug black trousers. I liked his drawly voice.

"Super accent," I said. "What is it?"

"I'm a Southern boy. Louisiana." He gave me a quick smile. "I like your accent too."

"I don't have one," I said. "It's you lot that do."

That got everyone talking about accents, a subject about which Gary, Maurice's partner, had a lot to say. Gary was quite a contrast to Maurice. Where Maurice was neat and reserved, Gary was rumpled and loud. His hair was longish and he had a rather untidy mustache. Gary more sprawled than sat, and he kept up a stream of comments, some of them witty. It wasn't that I didn't like him—he seemed pleasant enough—but he was one of those people who just have to be the center of attention.

Lucky for him, Maurice didn't appear to mind, being content to sit quietly and look at him affectionately every now and then.

When we went to the table, Gary insisted on helping Beth serve the meal. "I'm a thwarted waiter," he declared, placing a plate in front of me with a flourish.

I peered at it, puzzled. It would be rude to ask what the hell it was, but I wasn't keen on eating something that looked like this without some idea of its composition.

"I'm doing a course in Italian cooking," Beth declared to the table. "This appetizer is *sformato di piselli e asparagi!*"

"Asparagus and pea flan," Harriet translated.

"It didn't quite come out like the illustration in my cookbook," Beth said with the first tentative smile I'd ever seen on her face.

This had to be an understatement. The contents of the plate in front of me appeared to be afflicted by some dire tropical skin disease. I looked around the table. Others were eating, and no one had fallen off a chair, as yet. I took an experimental mouthful. It tasted OK.

Gary rushed around, pouring red Italian wine. Then he whisked away the appetizer plates from each of us. If he loved being a waiter, why wasn't he one? I was curious enough to ask him what he did.

"Teacher," he said. "Math."

"With LAUSD," said Harriet in tones of doom.

"What's that?"

"Los Angeles Unified School District," said Gary, topping up Beth's glass. She was drinking quite a lot, I'd noticed. Maybe it was anxiety about her cooking.

"Anyone who teaches in L.A. Unified deserves a medal," Harriet declared. "There are too many chiefs, not enough Indians, dilapidated buildings, and a large proportion of students who are functionally illiterate in English. Oh, and there's gang violence too."

"Gary's a wonderful teacher," said Maurice, "but he's close to burning out."

My opinion of Gary went up several notches. Teaching was a demanding profession at the best of times. In Gary's situation, it sounded close to impossible.

Beth, her forehead creased in concentration—or maybe panic—exited to deal with the main course. Gary followed after her. We were chatting about red wine versus white when a few horrified cries filtered through from the kitchen. "Stay here," said Harriet, getting up.

"Sounds like there's a problem with the entrée," Chantelle said.

"Entrée? We've already had the entrée."

Maurice and Chantelle looked at me. "The first course," I told them. "The asparagus and pea thingy."

"That's the *appetizer*," said Chantelle. "Now we're waiting for the main course. The entrée." She grinned at me. "You Aussies are so strange. Must be something to do with living upside down at the bottom of the world."

"Entrée means entry," I pointed out. "So it's the first thing you have."

Maurice frowned at me. "If you Aussies call the appetizer the entrée, what do you call the main course?"

"Funnily enough," I said, "the main course."

Harriet came in from the kitchen. "Beef filet with truffles and apples," she announced. I could she was on the verge of hopeless giggles but was attempting to remain serious for Beth's sake.

Beth and Gary entered, carrying plates. Beth was unsmiling. *"Filetto con tartufi e mele,"* she said without her usual verve.

My mum has a saying about Aunt Millie's cooking—not to her face of course. "When Millie cooks," Mum would declare, "it's either a burnt offering or a bloody sacrifice."

I examined my main course. On my plate sat my very own burnt offering.

CHAPTER TEN

As soon as I saw Melodie's gloomy expression Monday morning, I assumed the Saturday callback hadn't gone well. "Missed out, did you?" I said, sounding as sympathetic as possible.

"Not at all," said Melodie. "That was the *first* callback. I expect to get a second callback later this week. Larry, my agent, says not to worry—he just knows they loved me."

First thing every Monday morning a meeting was held in Ariana's austere office to report on all current cases. Everyone was expected to attend, except for Melodie and Fran. Up to this point I'd really only been a spectator, but now, even if I were under Bob Verritt's supervision, I had a case of my very own.

I'd found it was traditional for Ariana to supply doughnuts for the meeting, although I suspected it pained her to have crumbs scattered all about by Lonnie, who, nice bloke though he might be, was an awfully messy eater.

Everyone trooped in with coffee, except me (I had a good strong cup of tea) and Harriet (who insisted on drinking a peppermint concoction made with a *BlissMoments* tea bag). We sat in a circle, with Ariana the focal point behind her desk.

Feeling incredibly pleased to be part of this group, I checked out my companions. Bob, thin as a rake, had folded himself onto his chair. Lonnie had dumped a stack of papers on the chair next to mine and had gone to inspect the selection of doughnuts in the cardboard box on Ariana's desk. Harriet, who took notes of these meetings and came up with an efficient two-page précis every week, was shifting around in her chair as though she couldn't get comfortable, probably something to do with being pregnant. Or maybe she just couldn't get comfortable. Ariana's furniture was rather severe, like Ariana.

I saved Ariana Creeling for last, just the same as I always saved the most delicious food for last, or the book I thought I'd enjoy the best, for last. My mum had never understood why I did it, and I never could explain to her why anticipating something made the pleasure better.

Ariana was sitting calmly behind her desk, very still, watching as people took their places. I remembered what a jolt her blue eyes had given me the first time I'd walked into her office. Familiarity hadn't diminished the affect at all. This morning, as she had been that first day, she was dressed all in black, and her pale blond hair was pulled back in a chignon.

Although Ariana was the same, my appearance had improved markedly. The day we'd first met, I'd been jet-lagged and wearing jeans and a T-shirt. This morning I had on a tailored navy suit and creamy silk blouse. And my new hairstyle still looked pretty good, even if I'd ruined Luigi's strenuous blow-drying by washing my hair under the shower, ignoring his advice on using a conditioner, and then letting it dry naturally.

After we'd all settled down, Ariana said, "I'd like to discuss a new client first, Nanette Poynter. There may be some impact on Bob and Kylie's Hartnidge case, as the problem she has involves Brother Owen of the Church of Possibilities."

"Nanette Poynter?" said Lonnie, spewing crumbs as he tried to swallow a mouthful of chocolate doughnut and talk at the same time. "The one who used to be Nanette Sullivan?"

"You want a serviette?" I said, handing him one of the flimsy paper ones that had come with the doughnuts.

He swallowed. "A what?"

"A serviette."

"We call them napkins."

Ariana frowned. We all came to attention. She said, "Yes, Lonnie, *that* Nanette Poynter."

"Trophy wife," said Harriet. "Used to be a model. Vernon Poynter's second, or is it third?"

"His third wife," said Lonnie. I guessed he must absorb everything available about the rich and famous, as he always seemed to know all about them. "She married him in her late twenties, but now she's pushing forty, rather long in the tooth for a trophy wife. Poynter himself's got to be in his eighties. You've got to wonder how he gets it up."

"You may not know, Lonnie," said Bob with a wicked grin, "but there's these little tablets…"

Lonnie snickered, then caught Ariana's eye. "Sorry."

"As Lonnie has pointed out," said Ariana, "Nanette Poynter is much younger than her husband. He's extremely rich, being the Poynter of Poynter and Yarnell, stockbrokers."

"What's the problem?" asked Harriet. "A prenuptial?"

Ariana shook her head—elegantly, of course. "Amazingly, no prenuptial agreement is in force. Apparently, against all advice, Vernon Poynter married her without one. What's worrying Nanette is that her husband has been sucked into the Church of Possibilities. Brother Owen is persuasive. He's got Poynter promising to give COP millions."

"There goes Nanette's inheritance," said Bob. "It doesn't seem fair, does it? She does her time in hell, and in the end doesn't get paid for it."

"Maybe she married him for love," I said.

Lonnie smothered a laugh. "Good one." Then he caught sight of my expression. "Kylie! Don't tell me you weren't joking!"

"Alzheimer's," said Harriet. "Have Vernon declared incompetent."

"That won't fly," said Ariana. "Poynter's recently had a full checkup and he's mentally and physically in great shape."

"So what's she want Kendall & Creeling to do for her?" I asked.

"Not much," said Ariana sardonically. "She only wants us to find evidence that will open her husband's eyes to the confidence game Brother Owen is playing, preferably before the last red cent of her inheritance disappears into the church's coffers."

We discussed the case for a good while, deciding Lonnie was to research COP's finances and Harriet was to investigate pending and past lawsuits against the "church."

Ariana said to me, "I'd like you to sit in on a meeting I have with Nanette Poynter this afternoon. It may be valuable background for your case."

My case. In my imagination I sang a line or two of "My Girl," substituting "My Case."

"Kylie?"

"That'd be bonzer, if it doesn't clash with Alf and Chicka's appointment. They're due here at four."

Before going to Ariana's office this morning, Bob had told me he'd spoken to Alf, and both brothers were all for me going undercover. They were coming over this afternoon to finalize the details.

"That'll work," said Ariana. "Nanette Poynter will be here at two."

Then we discussed my case, my case—the song kept ringing in my ears like an endless audio loop. Lonnie gave us the results of his preliminary background checks of the Oz Mob staff. As he said he'd expect in any group like this, he'd turned up minor criminal records for some of them—drunk driving, possession of small amounts of drugs, and one domestic violence arrest.

However, there were three people of special interest. As well as Tami Eckholdt's sister, Patsy, working under a false name, Ira Jacobs and Ron Udell had apparently given up very senior positions in the Church of Possibilities to take lower-paying jobs with the Hartnidges' company.

"What did they do in the COP organization?" I asked.

"Ira Jacobs is an accountant, previously handling large sums of money for the church," said Lonnie. "Ron Udell was a hotshot in PR. Neither was fired."

"They've got to be there for some reason," Bob said.

"I've got to dig deeper," said Lonnie. "I'm sure there's much more about these guys, but it's well hidden, which is suspicious in itself."

I looked over at Harriet, who, even though she hadn't yet passed the bar exam, was really sharp about the law. "Harriet, what happens if Alf and Chicka violate the morals clause in their contract with Lamb White?"

"I'd have to see the contract, but at a guess, I'd say the movie deal would fall through for sure, plus there'd be a severe monetary penalty of some sort."

"You mean the Hartnidge brothers would be up for damages?"

"Considerable."

"Enough to wreck their company?"

Harriet pursed her lips. "Could be. I'd need to know their financial situation. They may be carrying insurance against such an eventuality."

"No insurance," said Lonnie. "I checked them out. Alf and Chicka are in a precarious financial position. They've put everything toward getting into the American market. If this deal with Lamb White falls through..." He made a throat-cutting gesture.

"Maybe that's it," I said to Ariana. "The smuggled opals may not be intended for sale here. What if their function is to trigger the morals clause?"

"Interesting scenario," said Ariana. "I suggest you and Bob follow up on it."

Speculations about the opals buzzed in my thoughts, so I hardly heard the rest of the meeting. I'd pick up anything important later in Harriet's notes, I told myself. Meanwhile, I'd concentrate on my case. My case.

"Are you singing something?" Lonnie hissed, looking at me as though I'd slipped a mental cog or two.

"I don't think so," I said, too loudly.

Everyone stopped talking and switched their attention to me.

"She was singing," said Lonnie.

I spread my hands. "What can I say? I'm a happy soul."

* * *

Later that morning, when I was in the kitchen, Fran stalked in and fixed me with an acid smile. "Well, if it isn't the songbird," she said. "What's your next selection to brighten up our lives? Something from *The Sound of Music?*"

Note to self: Strangle Lonnie.

I kept out of everyone's way until two o'clock, when Nanette Poynter was due in Ariana's office. I was there right on time, but she hadn't arrived. This gave me an opportunity to explain to Ariana.

"You know how Lonnie said I was singing this morning in the meeting?"

"Uh-huh." She seemed amused.

"I know I'm going to sound like a bit of a drongo, but it was because of my case."

"Is a drongo worse than a galah?" Ariana inquired.

"A drongo's *really* stupid—a galah's just a fool."

"I see." She looked solemn, but I was pretty sure she was laughing at me.

This was uphill work, but I forged ahead. "There's this song, 'My Girl.' You know the one?" I sang a line, to make sure she did. Ariana nodded. Her lips were beginning to curve.

"So this morning, when you referred to the Hartnidge case, as 'my case'"—to make things clear, I pointed at myself—"for some reason it made me think of that song. And then the tune kept repeating in my head, and before I knew what was happening, I sort of hummed along with it."

She bent her head and covered her eyes.

Concerned, I said, "Crikey, Ariana, it's not that bad is it?"

She was still laughing when she answered the buzz of her phone. "Ms. Poynter's here? Send her in."

Nanette Poynter was, not surprisingly, a blond. A skinny blond. I reckoned these two things were probably required of anyone aiming to become a trophy wife. She moved like the model she once had been, with that odd leading-with-the-hips sort of walk, as if she were on an invisible fashion runway.

Ariana ushered her to the comfortable black leather client chairs nested around a white marble coffee table. There were only two lounge chairs, so I moved over one of the spindly ones for myself.

Nanette Poynter glided to her plumply upholstered chair and lowered herself into it with one smooth motion. She sat with her feet together, angled to one side. Her hands, neatly clasped, were placed on her knees. Her spine was straight, her shoulders held back, her head one-quarter turned. I figured when no one was there to look at her she most likely sprawled all over the place, with a glass of gin in one hand and a cigarette stuck in the corner of her mouth. However, with an audience, she was a proper lady.

Ariana introduced me as, "My colleague, Kylie Kendall."

Nanette Poynter inclined her head in my direction but didn't speak. She was very good-looking in a glossy sense. Everything was smooth—her hair, her skin, her facial expression. Her jewelry was discreet but undoubtedly very expensive. She was like a beautiful life-size doll.

"Would you mind outlining the situation again, Ms. Poynter?" Ariana asked.

"Please call me Nanette. I don't stand on ceremony."

Her voice was a surprise. I was expecting a softly modulated tone to go with her appearance. Instead it was rather raspy, with a querulous note.

"Thank you, Nanette. I'm Ariana."

"In a nutshell here's the situation. My husband, Vernon, has never had time for anything even vaguely spiritual. When I married him he was hard-nosed and by-the-numbers. Then last year he fell into the clutches of that asshole, Brother Owen, and his cockamamie religion. In a few months he went from a strong, no-nonsense character to a pathetic weakling who totally believes the hogwash the Church of Possibilities is pushing. That includes the neat idea that anyone who criticizes COP is in league with dark forces."

I was fascinated. Nanette's voice was full of emotion, but her face remained almost expressionless.

"Can you believe it?" she went on. "A tough, down-to-earth man like Vernon Poynter is sucked into what is so plainly a scheme to strip him of his money. *My* money."

"Have you seen the COP Web site?" I asked. "It's impressive from a psychological point of view, very cleverly playing on the feeling many people have that they're not fully appreciated, not understood."

"What hooey!" Nanette Poynter snorted, loudly. Her face remained impassive.

Ariana took Nanette through the process Brother Owen's organization had taken to ensnare Vernon Poynter. I wrote down all the names she mentioned, both the COP staff and the members of the congregation Nanette knew. It was startling how many celebrities even I, a stranger in L.A., recognized. The Church of Possibilities had to be raking in a fortune every week.

At the end of the session, Ariana accompanied Nanette Poynter to the parking area. I tagged along too. Nanette model-walked to her car, a huge Bentley. It was a horrible brown color, with gold insignia. She slid into the seat, legs outside, feet together, slanted appropriately. Then, with one deft movement, she was in a driving position. Dark glasses on, she turned her blank face in our direction. "I'll hear from you soon?"

"We'll be in touch," said Ariana.

The Bentley purred out into the Sunset Boulevard traffic. I said, "She never had much expression on her face, did she?"

"Botox."

"Botox does that? I thought it was just for wrinkles."

"Used cosmetically, it paralyzes small facial muscles, and that removes lines," said Ariana. "It also smooths character out of your face. Some women have had so much in their foreheads, they can't lift their eyebrows."

I grinned. "Clearly, you haven't had Botox injections."

She raised one eyebrow. "Thank you, I think." Her tone was dry.

"I don't mean you have wrinkles," I said hastily. "You don't need Botox. And you can raise your eyebrows really well." I stopped to regroup. "What I mean is…"

"I'd quit while I was ahead," said Ariana.

CHAPTER ELEVEN

The Hartnidge twins, plus me and Bob Verritt, were in my office. Alf and Chicka wore blue jeans and identical T-shirts, each bearing the words OZ MOB over a cartoon of an insanely grinning kookaburra.

I glanced around my office with satisfaction. It had originally been my father's room before he died. On my desk was a photograph of Dad and me when I'd been a little girl. It had been taken when my parents had still been married and living in Los Angeles. Sometimes I liked to think Dad was still here in his office, watching over me. For that reason, I didn't like to change it too much, for fear he wouldn't feel at home.

The charcoal-gray carpet was the same, as were the gray metal desk, bookcase, and filing cabinets. To lift the somber tone a little I'd had twelve of my best wildlife photographs framed and arranged on one wall. I was really proud of those close-ups of birds, reptiles, and animals in the bush around Wollegudgerie. Photography was the one area where I had infinite patience. I could look at each of my photos and place where and when it had been taken.

"I like the jacky," said Alf, indicating a shot I'd got just after dawn one morning of a kookaburra whacking a small snake against a branch to kill it.

"Laughing jackass is another name for a kookaburra," I said to Bob, in case he needed to be reminded.

He didn't want to know. "Let's get to work," he said. "What's the cover we'll use to get Kylie into the Burbank office?"

"I'm thinking girlfriend," said Alf.

Chicka nodded. "Girlfriend would do it."

"Wasn't the idea that you were going to give me a job in the company?" I said. "That way I could snoop around on the sly."

"Nah," said Alf. "A stickybeak girlfriend should do it. That sort of sheila always has her nose in other people's business. I'll let slip I'm dating an Aussie I tripped across here in L.A. and that I'm headover-heels for her."

"One prob," I said. "I'm a lesbian. I've never had a boyfriend. I'd really have to struggle to act the part."

Alf slapped me on the back. "No worries, love! Myself, I'm bi, so I see it from both sides of the fence. You'll be right, trust me."

He must have picked up my speculative glance in Chicka's direction, as he added, "Not Chicka. He's the straight one in the family. Aren't you mate?"

Chicka blushed and bobbed his head. "You could say that."

"Lucky for Melodie, eh?" Alf slapped me on the back again. "Chicka's a devil with the ladies, you know."

Chicka blushed a deeper pink.

Impatient with all this chitchat, Bob said, "We need to go through the logistics. Where Kylie's supposed to live, what her cover story is, where you're supposed to have met up. All that stuff."

"She'll be apples," Alf declared.

"He means everything will be OK," I translated for Bob. He didn't look convinced.

Alf gave me a big, toothy smile. "How's about it, Kylie? You free tonight for a nosh-up?"

First Ariana, now me? "A dinner date? We don't need to practice, Alf. I can play your girlfriend in the office."

Chicka threw back his head and hooted. "Kylie thinks you're putting the hard word on her, mate."

"Jesus," Bob muttered. "I wish someone would speak English around here."

"Putting the hard word on is asking for sex," I said to Bob.

Bob glared indignantly at Alf. "May I remind you this is a professional relationship between Kendall & Creeling and your company. Sexual favors are *not* included."

"I wasn't asking for sex," Alf declared. He winked at me. "Not that I'd turn her down if Kylie here wanted to try it with a bloke."

"No, thank." I said.

Alf put on a serious face. "Tonight's business, not pleasure. Tami Eckholdt of Lamb White is throwing Chicka and me a barbie to get together with some of her people." He jabbed a thumb in my direction. "Perfect op, don't you think? Kylie can come as my date. That gives her an in with the Lamb Whiters, doesn't it?"

Bob had to agree it did.

We got all the details straight, then Alf and Chicka got up to go.

"Chicka," I said, "can I ask you a serious question?"

He looked wary. "What question would that be?"

I was pretty sure he was stringing Melodie along. I didn't want her embarrassed. She was already telling all her friends she had a guaranteed part as a puppet voice. The longer it went on, the worse it would be.

"Did you offer Melodie a part in your Oz Mob movie?" I expected him to say no, and was poised to read all the signals he was lying.

Alf scowled at his brother. "Chicka, are you doing this *again?*"

Chicka got red. It must be a trial to blush that easily. "I might have mentioned something like that to Melodie," he said.

I was getting quite riled. "It's not right to get Melodie's hopes up that way." I was pleased to see that Bob's expression was irate too.

Alf patted my shoulder. "Don't get het-up, love. If Chicka's promised it, she's got the part." He frowned ferociously at his brother. "But this is the last time you do this, Chicka. All right?"

Chicka wilted a bit. "All right," he said.

* * *

I could see one looming problem that I hadn't mentioned to Bob or the Hartnidge brothers. After they'd left my office, I called Chantelle.

"Good afternoon! United Flair. How may I assist you?"

"It's me. This call is business, not pleasure."

"I'll hide my disappointment as best I can."

I loved Chantelle's sense of humor, but this was no time for light conversation. "Do you know the receptionist at Lamb White, the movie company?" I asked.

"Sure do. Rachelle's her name. Excitable type. I've never met her, but we've often spoken. The talent agents here frequently have clients auditioning for parts in Lamb White movies."

"Here's my situation," I said. "I know how incredibly efficient the receptionist network is."

Chantelle murmured approval of my assessment. Everyone likes to be praised.

"So—"

"Hold on, Kylie. Call coming through…Good afternoon! United Flair. How may I assist you?"

Chantelle took several calls, one after the other, then came back to our conversation. "You were saying how efficient receptionists were…"

"That efficiency may be a problem. This is absolutely between us, Chantelle. Top secret. Confidential. Hush hush—"

"Honey, I get the picture!"

"I'm going undercover for a case—"

"No! Like last time?" I'd met Chantelle during my first attempts at learning private eyeing, so she knew I'd had somewhat of a rocky start.

"I hope things will go much smoother."

"Amen," said Chantelle with a giggle.

"Can we be serious for a moment? I'm worried the receptionist at Lamb White will realize who I am. I reckon everybody on the network got an earful about what happened last time."

"You can relax," said Chantelle. "Rachelle's new in town. Just moved here from the Midwest. She's playing in the big leagues now and still trying to get up to speed."

"So if a little Aussie broad called Kylie turned up, Rachelle wouldn't make the connection?"

"No way," said Chantelle with certainty. "Besides, Rachelle's not the sharpest pencil in the box. She's nice enough but tends to get flustered."

I'd picked up from Chantelle and Melodie that receptionist flusterdom was judged very harshly. It was unprofessional to lose your head, whatever crisis came up.

"I'd speak to Melodie, if I were you," Chantelle advised. "She's your weak link."

"Melodie's a weak link?"

"Normally, she's very professional," Chantelle hastened to say. "Lately, however, Melodie's head's been turned with her tooth-whitening callbacks. And now the puppet voicing. She'd never mean to give you away, Kylie, but there's always an outside possibility."

"Melodie's got a second callback for the tooth commercial?"

"Just a few minutes ago," said Chantelle. "We're all very happy for her."

Armed with this information, I wasn't surprised to find Melodie on the phone, the air around her head thick with exclamations. "Amber! It's happened! The second, the *final* Refulgent callback! Larry, my agent, is over the moon! Damn. Another call coming through. Hold on, Amber…Good afternoon. Kendall & Creeling...Courtney! I got it! The final Refulgent callback!"

I cleared my throat.

"Gotta go, Courtney. Get back to you...Amber? Sorry, gotta go. Call you later."

"Congratulations, Melodie," I said. "That's wonderful news."

"It is, isn't it?" Melodie clasped her hands and did her looking-at-the-ceiling thing. "You slave to perfect your craft, and then your One Big Chance comes along and makes it all worthwhile."

"So you'll be leaving Kendall & Creeling?"

Melodie stared at me, amazed. "Haven't you heard the saying, 'Don't give up your day job?'"

I had, but it didn't seem something Melodie would apply to herself. "Isn't that advice for people who aren't very good?"

"It's true, I *am* good," said Melodie, "but until the residuals start rolling in, I won't consider myself secure enough to give up this job."

"Speaking of which," I said, "I've something to discuss, but it's off the record, not to be disclosed, confidential—"

"I get it, Kylie!"

I explained the situation. Melodie listened with close attention...or perhaps she was acting like she was paying attention.

Whatever, she kept her big green eyes on me until I'd finished, then said, "You've got another problem."

"I have?"

"The Church of Possibilities. They own Lamb White." I wasn't surprised Melodie knew this, not only because she'd been dating Chicka, but because I'd take bets she was familiar with every film company, every producer, every director in Los Angeles.

"It's Lamb White I'll be dealing with," I pointed out.

"Maybe so," said Melodie, "but I happen to know the church keeps a very close eye on everything." When I raised my eyebrows, she added, "Nicole, the receptionist before Rachelle, told me. It drove her mad."

I had to ask. "What happened to Nicole?"

"Married a COP missionary and moved to the Cook Islands." Melodie shook her head. "Such a waste. Basic phone system only."

* * *

Tami Eckholdt, head of Lamb White, had avoided being famine thin, which was a change. She had an athlete's body, tight and well-muscled. She wasn't tall, but she looked resilient, as though you could knock her down and she'd get right up again.

"Hello," she said, eyeing me with open curiosity. Her very short hair was a metallic copper that couldn't possibly have been natural.

"My girlfriend, Kylie," said Alf, a proprietary arm around my shoulders. He gave me a squeeze hard enough to bruise. "Knew you wouldn't mind if I brought her along."

"Not at all." Tami flashed a very white smile, fully worthy of a Refulgent girl, though in her case I reckoned it was probably a cosmetic dentist's work. She didn't seem the do-it-yourself type. She took my hand. "I'm sorry. I didn't get the name?"

"Kylie." We'd decided it would be easier to stick to my real moniker, although if anyone asked, my last name was going to be Kennedy, not Kendall.

"Welcome, Kylie." She linked her arm through mine. "Alf can look after himself for a while. Let me introduce my wonderful Lamb White team."

The patio we ended up on was crowded with people talking loudly. At one end, chefs in full getup, including those white, puffy hats, labored over two huge gas barbecues. My stomach rumbled. Lunch had been yonks ago.

"March, this is Kylie. Kylie, March is one of our wonderful directors." March flicked a look at me and lost interest immediately. "And this is…"

In no time flat, I was dizzy from names. It wasn't that I failed to pay attention—it was Tami Eckholdt's machine-gun delivery.

Spying another guest arriving, Tami said, "Steve will look after you, Kylie," and handed me off to a weedy bloke with big teeth, too large for his mouth. He had slightly protruding eyes and a prominent Adam's apple. He made me nervous by looking around all the time in an overanxious manner, as though everything we were saying was being recorded for later examination.

I was rather hoping to head for the barbecue area, but as no one else appeared to be eating yet, I advised my stomach to stop complaining and turned my whole attention to the weedy bloke. To start the ball rolling, I said, "You work for Lamb White, Steve?"

"I'd describe myself as Tami's right-hand man."

I couldn't think of a suitable rejoinder to this, so I kept quiet. An uneasy silence fell between us. Finally, I broke it with, "This place is really something."

I'd hit the conversational jackpot. Steve was delighted to show me the house and grounds while keeping up a running commentary. I'd realized this part of Rexford Drive in Beverly Hills was exclusive, but, Steve said, in COP's catalogue of buildings, this one was a jewel. The building's style, Steve told me authoritatively, was French provincial tweaked for American tastes. In short order, I knew more about French provincial architecture than I'd ever intended.

If the front of the place was imposing, the backyard was even more so. It had been elaborately landscaped as a sort of miniature Versailles gardens, Steve declared, a small version of the famous grounds where Marie Antoinette used to stroll.

"Why in the world would you copy Versailles in Beverly Hills?" I asked.

Steve stared at me. No one, he assured me, had ever asked him that question.

I was rescued from Steve by Alf, who flung his arm around my shoulders yet again and gave me another hard squeeze. I made a note to speak to him about that. "Kylie, old love," he boomed, "was wondering where you'd got to. Come and meet Rachelle. She's a ripper sheila."

Rachelle was almost certainly the new Lamb White receptionist. She turned out to be a breathless brunette with an impressive cleavage and masses of dark, curly hair.

"That Alf's such a card!" she squealed, as he was claimed by Tami and whisked away from us.

"Alf is one of a kind."

"One of a kind? Oh, that's so perceptive of you!"

Perhaps she always spoke in exclamations. I gestured toward the champagne she held.

"Nice champagne?"

"Nice! Oh, yes, of course! Cristal!"

"And that's good?"

She tinkled a laugh Melodie would have envied, then nudged me with her elbow, surprisingly hard. "Oh, *you*!"

I signaled to Chicka, who was standing forlorn with a champagne glass clutched in one large hand. "Over here, Chicka."

"Omigod!" exclaimed Rachelle. "Am I seeing double?"

Chicka came over and smiled down her cleavage. "G'day."

"You're twins, you and Alf!"

Chicka conceded that they were.

He looked astonished when Rachelle nudged him in the ribs the way she had me. She should register that elbow as a lethal weapon. "Omigod!" she shrieked. "You know what they say about twins!"

Alas, I was never to know what the word on the street was about twins, as Tami Eckholdt had turned up again. "Sorry to drag you away, Kylie, but there's someone Alf insists you meet. Someone special."

On these last two words her voice took on a reverent tone, so I wasn't too surprised to find a face familiar from the Web site. Brother Owen.

Alf was standing beside Brother Owen, and from his expression, was rather impressed by the man. I could imagine why he might be. Brother Owen did have an aura about him. Or maybe it was his cologne. I could smell a faint, musky scent.

He wasn't in his flowing white televangelist robes today but in a beautifully cut dark suit. Brother Owen's tie, I noticed, had little trumpet-blowing cherubs woven into the design. As he had on television, he looked sleek and well-fed. His neck bulged a little over the collar of his shirt, and the superb tailoring of his suit didn't quite disguise the extra weight he was carrying.

"God bless," Brother Owen said in a velvety bass voice. He put out his hand. His skin was soft and somehow creepy. Not sure whether I was supposed to bob a curtsy or maybe even kiss the fat emerald ring on his finger, I decided to shake his hand instead. "G'day. I'm Kylie."

"An Australian," he said approvingly. "Yours is a wonderful country."

"You've been Down Under?"

He smiled. Standard sparkling teeth, of course. "As it happens, just in the past few months, my dear. The Church of Possibilities is setting up a ministry in Australia."

Now this was interesting. "Really?" I said. "Where in Oz?"

"We're examining several sites, in both urban and country areas."

"Have you heard of Wollegudgerie?" I asked. "Alf and Chicka's family live near there. Opal-mining town."

"Wollegudgerie? I don't believe I ever have."

My *Complete Handbook* was quite stern about relying on gut feeling alone, but I was sure, absolutely sure, Brother Owen was lying.

CHAPTER TWELVE

My Aunt Millie arrived in Los Angeles late on Wednesday morning. I was at the international terminal at LAX to greet her. She wasn't hard to spot. She came out of customs pushing her luggage cart so pugnaciously that even seasoned travelers scattered before her.

I waved with as much enthusiasm as I could muster. "Aunt Millie. Over here."

She steered in my direction, narrowly missing an Italian family noisily reuniting. Aunt Millie was usually a ball of belligerent energy, but today she seemed subdued, tired. There was none of the usual fire in her voice as she looked me up and down and then declared, "You've lost weight. Doesn't suit you. Need meat on your bones."

"You look exactly the same, Aunt Millie."

And she did. Short, stocky, cantankerous. Her skin, still smooth and soft, was a much darker shade than mine. Her hair was graying, but her eyes were the same beautiful liquid brown. Right now they were squinting at me critically.

"Are we going to stand here all morning?"

I indicated no. We set off for the parking structure with me pushing the luggage cart and my aunt stomping along beside. "Good flight?" I inquired.

"Good? You're asking someone who's spent hours cooped up in a metal cylinder, squashed into a tiny airline seat, if it was good?"

I sighed. My chats with Aunt Millie rarely went swimmingly. "Did you manage to get any sleep?"

My aunt snorted. "Oh, yes, slept like a baby," she said with deep sarcasm. "Who wouldn't, with people clambering over you every five minutes to go to the loo, or trying to start idiot conversations?"

I spared a moment to send a sympathetic thought to Aunt Millie's traveling companions. They would quite possibly be vowing never to fly again.

We came to my boring rental car. Aunt Millie regarded it without favor. "Thought you'd have a convertible, Kylie. What's the point of living in Southern California if you don't have a convertible?"

"I can't imagine what I was thinking. I'll rush right out and get one."

That got a glimmer of a smile from Aunt Millie. Fortunately, underneath her snarl there lurked at least a ghost of a sense of humor.

"You do that," she said. "And make sure it's red. I like red cars."

She did actually, having a rather battered red sedan herself. My mum always said it was fortunate her sister had chosen a bright color, as Millie was the world's worst driver and people needed to see her to get out of her way.

"I'm taking you straight to your hotel, so you can freshen up," I said, darting into a tiny break in the traffic that seemed to roar around and around LAX's many terminals in an unending loop of frustrated drivers.

"You're not taking me to meet those Kendall & Creeling people you'd rather be with than your own family?"

"I'm saving that for later."

When we made it to the freeway, it was, as always, clogged with vehicles. "Humph. The traffic's worse than the last time I was here," my aunt observed. "*Much* worse."

I looked at her in surprise. I had no idea she'd ever visited the States. I knew she'd been to Fiji with her husband, Uncle Ken, before he died, but I couldn't remember her traveling much more than that.

"I didn't know you'd been here before, Aunt Millie."

"Ken and I visited your mother when she was married to Colin and living here in L.A. I'm surprised you don't remember. You cried every time you set eyes on me."

"I wonder why," I said, hiding a grin. Obviously even at an early age I'd recognized a noxious relative.

My aunt sniffed. "Ken liked it here. Got carried away with all those film stars living nearby. Insisted on wandering around with a star map looking for their houses, until I put my foot down."

My mother contended that Uncle Ken had died to get away from Millie. I recalled being quite shocked the first time Mum had said this, but I had come to see it as a real possibility.

"How's Brucie?" I inquired politely. We might loathe each other, but he *was* family.

"He's doing all right." She glanced over at me with a fearsome glare. "You're not to put ideas in Brucie's head that you want him over here. He's like his father—a hopeless romantic."

I couldn't help smiling. Cousin Brucie didn't have a romantic bone in his body.

"Smile away, Kylie! Brucie's saving his money to buy a plane ticket."

My smile disappeared.

"He even had the hide to ask me, his mother, to fund his wild ideas. I told him, Brucie, your place is here in Wollegudgerie with your own kin, not gadding about with strangers."

For once, I felt the need to stand up for my cousin. "I'm his kin, too," I said.

"You're half American," snapped Aunt Millie. "Your father was nice enough to me, but he was basically unstable, like Yanks in general. It's no wonder you lobbed over here without a word to anybody. It's in your genes."

Now I was getting angry. She could criticize me all she wanted, but I wasn't going to hear anything against my father. "Please don't talk about Dad that way."

With a grudging nod, she said, "Fair enough. You're loyal. I'll give you that, Kylie."

Uh-oh. I held my breath.

"Loyal, except to your mother. You've been disloyal there, my girl, leaving her in the lurch that way, with the pub to run and Jack O'Connell being worse than useless."

"Jack and Mum are going to be married. It's a case of three's a crowd. I would have moved out anyway and probably left the 'Gudge for Sydney or Brisbane."

"I wouldn't bank on the marriage," said my aunt darkly. "Like most men, Jack's more trouble than he's worth."

"Mum's told you they're breaking up?"

"Not in so many words, but I know which way the wind is blowing. If Jack doesn't stop throwing his weight around, he'll be out on his ear."

"Mum told me she loves him."

"*Love*! In the long run it never leads to anything good. Addles your brains and ruins your common sense. I've no time for it."

She gave me her best piercing look. It made my skin tingle. "You're not in love, Kylie, are you? That's not what's keeping you here, is it?"

"Of course not," I said, thinking of Ariana's blue, blue eyes.

Aunt Millie grunted, a singularly nasty sound. "Of course everybody in the 'Gudge knows Raylene threw you over for that hairdresser, but I can't believe you're staying away just because of that."

"I inherited half of Dad's business here in L.A., Aunt Millie. That's what's keeping me here."

"Fifty-one percent, if I'm not mistaken. Controlling interest." Aunt Millie had always been sharp as a tack over anything financial. That gave me an idea.

"Aunt, why don't *you* help Mum with the Wombat's Retreat? You've always been terrific with anything to do with money."

Silence. I looked over to see why. Her face was squinched in a thunderous scowl. "Aunt Millie?"

"I offered," she ground out. "Your mother turned me down flat. I have no idea why."

I did.

* * *

The accommodation I'd booked for my aunt was a mid-range hotel off the Sunset Strip and deliberately not within walking distance of Kendall & Creeling, unless you wanted a long slog uphill.

I'd originally suggested a motel as a less expensive alternative, but my aunt had been convinced the odds were any motel situated near the infamously sinful Sunset Strip was likely to be a house of ill repute, frequented by individuals with corrupt sexual appetites. She wanted none of that, thank you.

I got her settled into the hotel and left her eyeing the mini-bar. Although she rarely drank alcohol, Aunt Millie was a great believer in the medicinal powers of brandy as a pick-me-up. I'd have mentioned to her brandy could also be quite a throw-me-down, especially when one was jet-lagged, but Aunt Millie never took advice, particularly from feckless nieces like me.

I'd hardly walked through the door at work before Melodie demanded, "Where's your Aunt Millie?"

"I left her back at her hotel."

"Bummer."

I regarded Melodie with deep suspicion. "Why do you want to know where my aunt is?"

Melodie blinked innocent green eyes. "No particular reason."

Lonnie came hurrying down the hall. I knew it was him before I saw him, because he favored one leg, just a little, so he had a very identifiable gait. "Is Kylie on her way back?" he called. Then he saw me. "Oh, hello. You're here." He gazed past me hopefully.

"Aunt Millie isn't with me," I said.

Usually Lonnie and I got on very well, but since I'd snarled at him on Monday because he'd gone and told Fran and Melodie about my singing during the meeting, he'd been rather distant.

"Kylie's left her aunt at the hotel," said Melodie.

"What's going on?" I demanded.

A sigh from Lonnie. "You might as well tell her."

Melodie tossed her head. "*You* tell her. It was your idea."

"Oh, all right," said Lonnie. "We've got a bet with Fran about your aunt."

"What kind of bet?"

"Fifty dollars says Fran can't be civil to your Aunt Millie for longer than thirty minutes. Time starts the moment they meet."

"And Fran agreed to this?"

"Would you believe it, she did!" Lonnie cackled. "Silly girl thinks she can control her essential nature."

He gasped when from behind him, Fran snapped, "Watch it! This silly girl will take you apart."

"I'm out of here," said Lonnie, scooting back the way he'd come.

Melodie and Fran both looked at me. "The earliest you'll see my aunt is tomorrow," I said. "After her long trip, she's very tired."

"Does music run in the family?" Fran inquired with a wicked smile. "Does your Aunt Millie sing to herself, too?" Fran wasn't one to let things go.

To the best of my knowledge, my aunt was tone deaf. "Opera," I said. "Lovely voice."

* * *

"Another shipment of Oz Mob toys has arrived," said Bob, coming into my office and folding himself up like a paint easel into a chair. "Chicka called in a panic. You weren't here, so I spoke to him."

"More opals?"

Bob nodded. "The Kelvin Kookaburras are loaded with them. Same as before, Chicka says. Good quality black opals."

At our advice, the Hartnidge brothers had rented a unit in a self-storage facility and were keeping all the toys shipped to them in that secure location. We had some of the smuggled gems in our safe in the offices, but it was more than likely that undetected stones were still concealed in the little bodies of other toys.

"I've been thinking," I said to Bob. "Maybe we should set a trap. Get Alf and Chicka to bring some of the Kelvin Kookas into the Burbank office and leave them there. Then see who acts suspiciously. Lonnie could set up a concealed video camera, couldn't he?"

"Nanny cams," said Bob. "Parents install them to check that the nanny minding their children isn't abusing the kids when no one's watching. We've handled a couple of cases recently." He grimaced. "Very upsetting."

"Crikey," I said, "people can be gross, can't they? Anyone who touches a kid should be shot."

My phone rang. It was Alf Hartnidge. "All set, love? I'll be picking you up in forty minutes, OK?"

We'd arranged for me to meet the Burbank Oz Mob staff this afternoon as Alf's girlfriend. He'd be playing the successful entrepreneur, mega keen to impress me with his business.

"How do I look?" I said to Bob. "Do I impress you as the sort Alf would have as a girlfriend?"

Bob gave me a long, critical examination. "Higher heels," he said. "And more makeup."

When I'd been shopping with Harriet a few weeks back, she'd persuaded me to buy one pair of really high heels, but so far I'd avoided wearing them, figuring I needed practice if I wasn't to sustain a serious ankle injury.

"High heels? You sure, Bob?"

"Yeah, I'm sure. A girlfriend of Alf Hartnidge's would wear high heels."

I rarely wore much makeup, so I was no expert, but I knew someone who was. I made for the reception desk.

"Melodie, I need some help with my makeup."

"Makeup?" She seemed astonished I'd need assistance in this area. "You don't wear makeup, Kylie. You *should*, of course, but you don't."

"I'm pretending to be Alf's girlfriend this afternoon, when I meet his staff. I need to look like she would look."

"How much time have I got?" said Melodie, hauling one of her voluminous makeup bags from under her desk.

I checked my watch. "About twenty-five minutes."

Melodie rolled her eyes. "That's cutting it fine, but you've come to the right person." She peered at my face. "Twenty-five minutes?" she said. "Even for me, it'll be a challenge."

* * *

Alf arrived five minutes early, just as Melodie was putting the last touches to my face. I left them talking about Chicka and the movie and bolted back to my room to grab the high heels. When I tottered back on them, Alf was saying, "It'll be Penny Platypus or Korinne Koala, or maybe Wendy Wallaby. Not sure yet, love. The rest of the cast hasn't been finalized. We're talking to Russell Crowe's people about getting him for Kelvin Kookaburra. No probs with the Aussie accent there."

Melodie batted her eyelashes at him. "Which is the biggest female part, Alf?"

"That'd be Penny Platypus, I reckon."

"Penny Platypus…" Melodie gazed at the ceiling. I had the thought it might be a good idea to put a sign up there, possibly reading, GET BACK TO WORK!

She let her breath out in a long sigh. "I'm focusing, focusing. I'm searching for the real essence of Penny Platypus. The essential platypus…"

Alf gazed at her, nonplussed.

"Do you even know what a platypus is?" I asked.

Melodie frowned, "Um…" The phone rang. She seized it like a drowning woman would a lifeline. "Good afternoon! Kendall & Creeling."

Out in the car park, I stopped to blink at the gigantic pink convertible sitting in the visitors' spot. "Where did that come from?"

"It's a vintage Cadillac," Alf said, sweeping open the passenger door with a flourish. "Got bored with the car I had, so I went for something a bit flashier. The bloke that rented me this specializes in unusual luxury cars. There was a gold Maserati I had my eye on, but this beauty was calling my name."

As we pulled out into the traffic, Alf said, "Watch the heads turn, old love, watch the heads turn."

And turn they did, although it may not just have been the pink Cadillac. Alf drove like a man possessed. "I like to put the pedal to the metal," he bellowed above the slipstream we were generating.

"I can see that," I shouted back, hanging on for dear life.

On Burbank Boulevard we mercifully hit heavy traffic, and Alf was forced to slow down. I took the opportunity of relative silence to say, "Alf, lay off those one-armed hugs you like so much. My biceps are black and blue. You don't know your own strength."

"Sorry, mate. Will do."

My cell phone hiccuped. It was Melodie. "Your Aunt Millie's on the line. She says she's rested and ready to go."

"Oh, hell," I said. "Tell her I'm on a job and that I'll call her back as soon as I can."

"A problem?" Alf asked.

"My Aunt Millie's in town."

He looked at me uncomprehendingly, then his expression changed. "Strewth! Not Millie Haggety?"

I nodded. "My Aunt Millie."

Alf looked as though he'd swallowed something very unpleasant. "Ah, jeez, love. I don't have to see her, do I? Last time

I ran into Millie Haggety was at our big family do at Chrissie.
I suppose you know she's a sort of distant cousin of ours by
marriage. Her hubby had Hartnidge blood somewhere."

"What happened?"

"We had words. That's all I'll say." He shook his head
despondently, then said, half to himself, "The world's just not
big enough to escape her, is it?"

CHAPTER THIRTEEN

The Oz Mob office was in a smallish, dun-colored building just off Burbank Boulevard. Alf plummeted down the driveway into underground parking and screeched to a halt in a spot too small to contain the whole length of the Cadillac. Getting out, I inspected the considerable overhang at the back, caused by a boot clearly large enough to transport several bodies without crowding.

"It's sticking out quite a way," I observed.

"No worries," said Alf. He gestured at the other parked cars. "No one here wants to get pink paint on their transport."

I could see what he meant. Most of the cars seemed very new and very pricy. "All leased," said Alf, leading the way to dusty concrete stairs. I wobbled along behind on my extremely high heels. "Part of the package to get good staff."

"You're paying all these leases? Isn't that expensive?"

"Technically, our Oz Mob company's picking them up. It was on Tami's advice."

"Tami of Lamb White?"

"That Tami. She personally recommended this crash-hot accountant, Ira Jacobs, and we snapped him up, quick smart. Ira's a wonder. Showed us how leasing was by far the best way to go. In fact, he's got everything financial humming along, both here and in Australia. Don't know how Chicka and I did without him."

"So he has considerable control over the company's money?"

Alf glanced over at me rather defiantly. "I know what you're going to say. You've warned us some of our staff might not be true blue, but I'm sure Ira's the genuine article. I'd know if he wasn't."

Ariana, Bob, and I had talked it over and decided to give the Hartnidges a general warning that we'd found indications that some of their staff could be plants. We weren't going to specifically name anyone until Lonnie came up with concrete evidence.

"Who did Ira work for previously?" I knew from Lonnie it was the Church of Possibilities, but Alf would be in the dark about that.

"Some film company in New York," said Alf vaguely.

"You don't know the details and still you hired him?"

Alf frowned at my critical tone. "Tami had her Lamb White people run a background check. Told me Ira was dinky-di." Reaching the top of the stairs, he put his hand on the latch of the heavy metal door bearing the sign FIRST FLOOR and looked at me searchingly. "Do you know any different?"

Alf didn't strike me as good at hiding his feelings. If I revealed Jacobs had lied about his past employment, I was pretty sure Alf would start glaring at the accountant suspiciously. It wouldn't help our investigation if the bloke got wind of the fact that Alf was on to him, so I said, "We're still digging. I'll get back to you when we've got something specific."

"Because," said Alf, pushing open the heavy door, "I wouldn't want to let Ira go. Top bloke in every way. You'll see what I mean when you meet him."

I followed him into a thickly carpeted area, partitioned off into many largish cubicles. The Oz Mob setup was too small to employ a receptionist, so I had no need to worry about the RN—as I now mentally referred to the receptionist network.

I readied myself to twitter, as I imagined a rather dim girlfriend would. Tugging at my too short skirt, I contemplated my legs. They did look good in heels, but the blasted things were just as challenging to walk in as I'd feared. I thanked the genetic gods for my strong ankles.

Apart from Ira Jacobs, there were two others I was interested in meeting. One was Patsy Eckholdt, Tami's sister, who was calling herself Paula Slade. The other was Ron Udell, who had done public relations for COP, but, like Ira Jacobs, had concealed this when joining the Hartnidges' company.

Alf was looking around, seemingly expecting something to happen. Apparently the something was Chicka. He suddenly popped out of one of the cubicles. "G'day," he said, then swallowed nervously. Beads of sweat trickled down his face.

Alf had confided to me earlier that Chicka suffered from stage fright. "But it's *me* playing the role," I'd said, "not Chicka."

"He feels he has an important supporting part. He's taking it very seriously. Even skipped breakfast this morning to practice."

Clearly, practice hadn't made perfect. As an audience arrived, namely a woman with a bunch of folders in her hand, Chicka fixed her with a desperate stare and blurted, "Look who's here. What a surprise. It's Alf with his girlfriend, Kylie."

The woman halted and glanced sourly from me, to Alf, to Chicka.

Chicka cleared his throat. "Alf, have you brought Kylie here to impress her with the office?" He paused to give me a lipsdrawn-back grin, so obviously false I had to change my involuntary giggle into a cough.

"Yes, Chicka," said Alf, apparently suddenly infected with the same bad-acting virus. "I *have* brought Kylie here to see the Oz Mob office, where we work."

Yerks! I had to put a stop to this fast. "I'm Kylie," I said to the woman, putting out my hand.

"Paula."

Ah! So this was Tami Eckholdt's sister, Patsy, acting a role, just like me. She didn't resemble Tami, except maybe around the mouth. She was taller and somewhat overweight, and wearing an unflattering beige pantsuit and scuffed flat shoes. Her lank, brown hair fell listlessly to her shoulders. She had heavy black-framed glasses with those thick lenses that oddly magnify the eyes.

"Could you tell me where the restroom is?" I didn't need a loo, but I wanted to get away to give Alf and Chicka time to get their act together—if, indeed, they could.

"Sure. Follow me."

Paula put the folders on a table and set off down a short hallway, me teetering behind her. With every step my admiration grew for all those women I saw every day wearing such extreme footwear. I visualized them striding along with such apparent ease, their high heels tap-tapping, expertly disguising the complex physical adjustments constantly necessary to prevent pitching forward on their noses.

"In here." Paula indicated a blue door distinguished by a small black silhouette of a figure wearing a bouffant dress.

"With women wearing pants so much these days, it isn't really relevant, is it?" I said, indicating the silhouette.

Paula gave me a funny look. "I wouldn't know. Can you find your own way back?"

As we'd taken scarcely six paces down the hall, I told her I thought I could. Paula clumped off. She was graceless, I decided...or a wonderful actor. That reminded me I was supposed to be acting the part of Alf's girlfriend.

I pushed open the door and entered a white-tiled room. A faint chemical flower scent permeated the air. The mirror above the wash basins was unforgiving. I gazed at myself with horror. Melodie had declared she'd make me up perfectly for the part I had to play, and like a fool I'd left it all to her. Alf arriving early had meant I didn't have time to check a mirror. Would that I had!

It was clear to me Melodie had envisaged Alf's girlfriend as a rough sheila, fast-living, and with a bad rep. Someone my

Aunt Millie would call a painted woman. I sighed to myself. It was too late to do anything about it, especially as Paula Slade has already seen me.

When I got back to where I'd left Alf and Chicka, I was relieved to find Chicka had disappeared. I put my arm through Alf's. "Darl, show me around," I said, trying for a brightly eager tone. It came out nauseatingly chirpy. This acting stuff was harder than it looked.

Alf swept me around the office, introducing me as we went. I fluttered my eyelashes madly, telling Jerry, Jean, Leroy, and Caleb how mega great it was to meet them. I'd given up on brightly eager and was trying simpering. It seemed easier.

"And this is Ira Jacobs," said Alf. "Ira's doing a bonzer job, getting rid of all that red ink and putting us well in the black."

Ira Jacobs didn't look like an accountant. He reminded me of a particularly smooth, upmarket salesman. He was of medium height, with a good head of dark hair, a nice body, and a firm handshake. "Kylie, what a pleasure to meet you!" He spoke so warmly and flashed his teeth so winningly, I could almost believe his delight was genuine.

My Complete Handbook had warned me about successful salespeople. The very job they did made them efficient liars. I looked at his feet. To catch Ira Jacobs out I'd need to watch for subtle movements in the lower half of his body.

I became aware that both he and Alf were looking in the direction of his feet too. "Is something wrong?" Ira asked, frowning.

"Your shoes," I said. "Italian, aren't they? I just love Italian shoes!"

"As a matter of fact they are." He was pleased with the compliment. I was pleased I'd got away with it.

We ran across Paula in one of the cubicles. She was poring over a computer screen, mouse in one hand. "Paula's taking care of all our shipments of stuffed toys and hand puppets," said Alf, clapping Paula's shoulder. I noticed she winced. Alf didn't mean to be rough, but he was.

"How totally fascinating, Alf," I burbled, peering at the screen, "but what are you going to do with all these toys?"

"They're going to Lamb White's marketing division," said Alf. "Tami called me this morning and asked me to airfreight several extra crates to L.A. as soon as poss. Paula's handling it all. Doing a wonderful job, aren't you, Paula?"

"I try," she said tonelessly.

The last person I was introduced to was Ron Udell. I'd assumed anyone who'd made a career in public relations, as he had, would be polished and well-dressed. I was wrong. Ron Udell seemed comfortable in his blimp body and baggy clothes. He needed a haircut and his nails weren't clean.

"Ron's our liaison with the various companies and their PR departments," said Alf. "I don't even pretend to understand what Ron does, but I believe he does it well."

Ron came across to shake my hand. He moved like someone thinner and leered at me like someone more attractive. "Alf's a lucky SOB," he said.

I removed my fingers from his damp, warm clasp. "Thanks. It's nice of you to say so."

Now that everyone had met me, and it had been clearly established I was Alf's girlfriend, I wanted out of there. Aunt Millie was weighing on my mind. I should call her at her hotel but decided to put off that dire moment until I got back to Kendall.

"What do you think?" asked Alf, once we'd roared up the ramp out of the underground parking and butted into the stream of traffic.

"I think you need an outside audit of the Oz Mob books." I mentally checked through the chapter on financial crimes in my *Complete Handbook*. "In fact, what you need is a forensic accountant."

"And that'd be?"

"An expert who's trained to detect criminal activity, cooked books, fraud. Someone who'll go through the Oz Mob finances looking for anything out of place. I could take a look myself and give you some idea if things aren't quite right, but you'd be better off with a real professional to tell you exactly what's going on."

I'd expected Alf to be at the least dismayed that a forensic accountant might be necessary, but instead I found him gazing at me with admiration. "You understand balance sheets and all that stuff?"

"Straight forward financial statements I understand— balance sheets, profit and loss. I did that side of Mum's business for years."

"Bloody hell," said Alf, accelerating to beat a red light, "that whole area's double Dutch to me. Lucky Chicka handles that side."

"Chicka?" I said. "Chicka handles the financial side of your business?"

Stone the crows. The situation was worse than I'd thought.

* * *

Alf dropped me back at Kendall & Creeling and zoomed into Sunset Boulevard to a chorus of outraged horn-blowing. My feet were killing me. I limped to the front door with a feeling of anticipation. I'd get my suffering feet out of these shoes, wash off my garish makeup, get changed into something comfortable, and relax with Julia Roberts for a few minutes before I reported to Bob on my visit to Burbank.

My anticipatory smile was wiped off my face by Melodie's first words. "Your Aunt Millie's here."

"What! I left her at the hotel."

"She caught a cab."

My stomach sank. "Where is she?"

"In the kitchen with Fran and Lonnie and Harriet." Melodie's bottom lip shot out in a pout. "*I'd* be in the kitchen with them, but Ariana's still here, so I'm stuck in reception."

"That's why you're called a receptionist," I said coolly. "You recept."

Melodie wasn't listening. "Lonnie says he'll time it properly, but I don't trust him. I should be there too."

"This is the bet you've got with Fran?"

"Fifty dollars." Melodie checked her watch. "It's been more than twenty minutes." She frowned. "I don't understand. Fran can't be pleasant that long to anybody. What's gone wrong?"

"Hold the fort," I said. "I'll find out."

Leaving Melodie gazing dejectedly after me, I made for the kitchen. There I found Fran leaning with her back against the counter, her attention on my aunt, who was perched on a tall stool. They were in animated conversation, ignoring the silent spectators—Harriet, Julia Roberts, and Lonnie, who kept referring furtively to his watch.

"Shhh!" hissed Lonnie when I came through the door. He beckoned to me urgently. "Don't interrupt. Three minutes, thirty seconds left."

"You're not sneezing," I whispered.

"What?"

I pointed to Julia Roberts, who was sitting nearby, apparently paying close attention to the dialogue between Fran and my aunt. "You're allergic, remember?"

Lonnie scowled at Jules. "Thanks to that damn cat, I've got antihistamine coming out my ears."

Harriet shushed us.

"Harriet's got a piece of the action," Lonnie murmured.

I tuned in to the conversation. Fran was saying, "You can't trust the assholes to get anything right."

Aunt Millie nodded vigorously. "Too true, too bloody true. Crooked as a dog's hind leg, the lot of them."

"Politicians," Lonnie whispered to me. "They've found a hatred in common."

"Corrupt SOBs," said Fran. "Despicable, contemptible media whores."

"Hypocritical buggers, boofheads, and dags."

I murmured to Lonnie, "They seem to be getting on rather well."

"Yeah, damn it."

"What are you two talking about?" said Fran turning around to glare at us.

"It's private," Lonnie declared.

Fran sniffed and turned back to my aunt. "Where were we?"

"Oh, shit!" said Lonnie. "The time's up!"

Fran smiled triumphantly at Harriet and Lonnie. "I'll expect payment in cash by tomorrow morning," she said in a voice too soft for my aunt to hear. "No excuses." They departed, grumbling. Julia Roberts stalked off too.

Fran said to my aunt, "Great meeting you, Millie. We must do this again some time."

"For an American, she's not too bad," said Aunt Millie after Fran had left, no doubt to give Melodie the unpleasant news about the bet. "Got her head screwed on the right way. None of this pie-in-the-sky stuff."

"You don't think Fran has a rather dark view of life?"

"Not at all. I'd call it realistic. Like me, she tells it like it is, and—" She broke off to peer at my face. "What are you playing at, my girl? You're painted like a prostitute?"

"It's makeup."

By now Aunt Millie had homed in on my short skirt and high heels. "Disgusting. Your mother would be shocked."

It was no use trying to explain. "I'll go and change."

"While you make yourself decent, I'll have a word with your business partner, the Creeling woman."

I went quite cold. "Aunt Millie, please—"

"I can't rely on you to tell me the truth, Kylie. This Creeling woman may be more forthcoming."

"Her name is Ariana," I said. "Not the Creeling woman. If you wait until I change—"

"I'd prefer to see her alone."

I looked at her, a feeling of impotence flooding me. When her mind was made up, my aunt was implacable. Nothing I did or said would make any difference.

Bob Verritt chose this moment to come into the kitchen. Aunt Millie smiled up at him. "This nice young man can show me to your partner's office."

"Would you mind, Bob?" I said.

I had to get out of there before Aunt Millie saw the tears welling in my eyes. I slipped off my shoes, and carrying them in one hand, hurried to my room, fortunately meeting no one on the way.

I never cried. I wasn't going to now.

The best thing was to keep busy. I cleaned my teeth, washed my face, and changed into jeans and a plain blue shirt.

In all my life, I'd never hated Aunt Millie, not even when she was at her most unkind, but I was close to hating her now. What was she saying to Ariana? My mind skittered around all the possibilities, none of them good.

I wasn't going to skulk around my room. I'd go and see what was happening. I checked my face in the bathroom mirror and tried a smile. It didn't work. Better to try for serious, low-key.

As I reached Ariana's office, Aunt Millie and Ariana came out through the door. "There you are," said Millie. "I'm ready for you to drive me back to the hotel."

"OK," was all I could manage, without revealing how upset I was.

I glanced at Ariana. I couldn't read her expression. What in the hell had Aunt Millie told her?

The trip back to the hotel was silent. Jet lag had obviously caught up with my aunt, as she was having trouble keeping her eyes open. I saw her to her room, found the room-service menu for her, told her I'd call her in the morning, and went back to my car.

I didn't want to return to Kendall & Creeling. Everyone would have left by now, and the rooms would be empty and sad. But Jules would be expecting her dinner, so I had to go back.

Ariana's dark blue BMW was the only car left in the parking area. I sat and stared at it for a few moments, debating whether to go in or leave. I didn't want to face her tonight.

It was an effort to get out of my car and walk to the front door. I took a deep breath and opened it. Perhaps I could dodge Ariana and go to my room without running into her.

"Kylie?"

So much for that hope. "Yes, it's me." I locked the door behind me. It was getting dark, and I was always aware that danger could lurk in the shadows.

Ariana came toward me with her lovely loose-limbed stride. "Would you like tea? Or maybe a stiff drink?"

"Tea would be good."

Predictably, Julia Roberts was waiting in the kitchen. Ariana switched on the electric kettle while I fed Jules. "You lucky cat," I said. "It's turkey tonight."

Jules attacked the turkey with her usual enthusiasm. "It's her favorite," I said to Ariana, just to fill the silence between us.

Going through the ritual of making tea soothed me. Ariana surprised me by saying she'd have some too. "Don't you prefer coffee?"

"I'll keep you company."

Ridiculously, her just saying that upset me. I blinked hard and fiddled around with the teapot and finally poured the tea. We sat side by side on tall stools, our mugs sitting on the counter in front of us.

"That's quite an aunt you have there," she said at last.

"You could say that." I swiveled around on my seat to face her. "Ariana, I'm so sorry. I don't know what Aunt Millie said to you, but…"

Hell, I was going to cry.

Ariana put an arm around my shoulders. "It's all right."

I fished around in my pocket for a handkerchief. "I'm sorry to be such a sook."

She smiled. Her eyes were so blue. I couldn't help it. I leaned forward and kissed her.

CHAPTER FOURTEEN

Fran leaned her diminutive form against the kitchen counter in an identical pose to yesterday's, when she'd been talking to my aunt. Her china-doll face with its creamy skin was really very appealing, I decided, at least when she wasn't scowling. At the moment she looked quite pleasant.

She chewed reflectively on the health-food bar she habitually ate for breakfast. "There's something about your aunt I like."

I looked moodily at my porridge. "Her worldview, perhaps."

"There's that," said Fran, "but there's something more. Something almost inexpressible." She paused to consider the matter, then said, "I have the same quality myself. No one's ever been able to define it."

"I'll have a lash at defining it," I said. "Any of these words strike a bell? Bleak, gloomy, doom-laden—"

"You never get it, Kylie," Fran snapped, a scowl darkening her face. "Frankly, you're not sensitive enough."

Melodie entered the kitchen in time to hear Fran's last words. "Speaking for myself, I feel particularly sensitive today,"

Melodie declared. "It's the final Refulgent callback." She shot a look at me. "In my *lunchtime*." I didn't comment.

"Jesus," said Fran, "if I hear the name Refulgent again, I'll scream." She pointed the remains of her health-food bar at Melodie. "With you it's Refulgent this, Refulgent that. Get over it!"

"Larry, my agent, says I've got nothing to worry about," said Melodie, blithely ignoring Fran's outburst, "that my Date With Destiny is secure, but the artist in me can't help sense the texture of the situation."

"The texture of the situation? What the hell does that mean?" Fran barked.

"Only an actor would understand, but I'll try to explain," said Melodie. "In layman's terms, it's the quality of the moment, the essential *thisness*, if you like, the being there."

Fran gave her a long, disgusted look, then said to me, "She's all yours, Kylie," and strode out of the room.

Melodie gazed after her. "You'd think Fran would be more perceptive, wouldn't you, being married to a writer." She shook her head. "I don't know how Quip puts up with her." I didn't either.

"Oh," said Melodie, "before I forget, the answering service had a message for you from your aunt."

I braced myself. I really, really didn't want to see her today. I had my excuses ready but knew only too well how difficult Aunt Millie was to deflect.

"She's going to Disneyland," said Melodie.

"Disneyland?" This was astonishing. My Aunt Millie in the Happiest Place on Earth? Surely there'd be cosmic consequences when ultimate angst met ultimate gladness.

"She's taking a tour arranged through the hotel," said Melodie. "Be gone all day."

Hallelujah!

"Right-oh," I said.

Melodie helped herself to coffee then left me alone with my porridge. I looked over to where Ariana and I had been sitting at the counter last night. Where I'd kissed her.

I could re-create vividly the texture of that situation, the quality of that moment. I'd kissed Ariana, and she'd kissed me back. Her lips had opened beneath mine. About this there was no doubt. I grew warm at the thought.

But then, as I had known she would, Ariana had pulled back. It seemed to me she'd broken our kiss with the same reluctance as I had. How I had wanted more, much more. And surely, so did she.

At some level I knew with absolute certainty that if I revealed the depth of my feelings, I'd irrevocably drive Ariana away. So I'd said nothing as she slid off the stool and stood beside me, her hand still on my shoulder, inquiring in a friendly tone if I were all right. It was as if the kiss had never happened. I'd nodded yes.

Ariana had paused, irresolute, and for a moment I believed she'd take me in her arms. But then she'd said we'd discuss my aunt in the morning, wished me good night, and left.

I hadn't thought I'd be able to sleep, that I'd lie awake, reliving the burning memory. Instead I fell into a deep sleep and dreamed. Dreamed of Ariana in my bed, until I awoke in the early morning, cold with disappointment to find myself alone.

* * *

"Your Aunt Millie," said Ariana, "actually believes I have the power to persuade you to sell me your share of Kendall & Creeling."

We were sitting opposite each other in Ariana's office, the wide black surface of her desk between us. She was, as usual, cool and controlled. "What did you say?" I asked.

"I pointed out there was no way I could persuade you to do anything you didn't want to do, and as you were determined not to sell, that was the way it was going to be. Then I observed it seemed to run in the family, this admirable intractability."

I had to smile. "You actually said admirable intractability?"

"I did, and your aunt seemed pleased to hear it. She admitted it was a quality she'd noticed in you before, and agreed it was, indeed, a family trait."

I knew what was coming next. "Then Aunt Millie mentioned my mother, didn't she?"

Ariana steepled her fingers and looked over them at me. "Your aunt maintains you're urgently needed to help run your mother's hotel. She mentioned duty more than once."

I winced. Aunt Millie knew the strings to pull for maximum effect. Her aim was to make me feel guilty for leaving Mum in the lurch. And it was working. I had qualms about staying away.

Ariana had been watching my face. "Be resolute, Kylie," she said. "Do what you want to do, not what others think you should."

"You don't think I'm resolute?"

"I think the family card is being played." Her tone was dry. "It's the high card in the pack, and it's a difficult one to resist."

We looked at each other across the desk. I said, flatly, "I'm staying in L.A."

Was that a quick flash of pleasure on Ariana's face? Perhaps I'd imagined it, because I was yearning to see it.

"Now the hard part," said Ariana, "is convincing Aunt Millie you really do mean what you say."

I nodded soberly.

* * *

I'd reported to Bob the details of my visit to Burbank, and we had agreed the time had come to have a strategy meeting with the Hartnidge twins and tell them everything we knew so far, which wasn't all that much.

Lonnie came in to our mini conference chomping on a fat cream bun. He finished it, leaving a trail of powdered sugar down his front. Licking his fingers, he reported he'd run into a dead end with his detailed background search for Ira Jacobs and Ron Udell. "This shouldn't happen," he told Bob and me. "Someone's gone to a lot of trouble to clean up these guys. It makes me wonder why."

We were sitting in Bob's office, which was rather messy, though not in Lonnie's clutter league. There was an old jukebox in one corner—I'd tried it and it worked—files all over the place, and a wall full of old movie posters. I admired the one for *Laura*. Gene Tierney had been a major babe.

"I'd like to know if either of these blokes have traveled to Australia recently," I said. "And would you check out Brother Owen at the same time? He told me he'd been Down Under in the past few months. If you could find out where he traveled internally, that'd be bonzer."

"Consider it done," said Lonnie.

After he'd brushed powdered sugar all over the place, Lonnie took himself off. I said to Bob, "Something's worrying me."

"Lonnie's diet?"

"Alarming though it is, no. We're breaking the law, aren't we, by not reporting those smuggled opals we've got in the safe to Customs, or to whatever other authorities should be involved?"

"We don't know they're smuggled. Not for sure," said Bob blandly.

"I thought ignorance was no defense in law."

Bob shrugged his narrow shoulders. "It'll fly."

"But—"

"Think this through, Kylie. There's absolutely no way the story will be kept quiet if the opals are reported. The Feds will be on it, some bright spark in Homeland Security will come up with the theory it's got something to do with terrorism, and so on. Alf and Chicka get to kiss the Lamb White movie goodbye, and worse, because of the draconian morals clause in their contract, they'll almost certainly be sued by the studio. Lonnie's already pointed out the Hartnidges are in a precarious financial position. This will ruin them. Get the picture?"

"I see what you mean," I said. "Our clients come first."

"Atta girl."

Alf and Chicka were due at ten, and as they were usually early for appointments, when ten came and went, I wondered what had happened. I went out to reception, thinking Melodie might have received a message and forgotten, in the excitement of her lunchtime Date With Destiny, to pass it on to me.

Chicka was there, in khaki shorts and shirt, both sporting multiple pockets. He was leaning over, talking to Melodie in agitated tones.

"What's up?" I said.

He turned an agonized face in my direction. "I walked here from the accident. It's down a block or so on Sunset Boulevard. Alf's still there."

"Is anyone hurt?"

"Just the pink Cadillac. It's got a pretty big ding. And so has the Hummer."

"The Hummer ran into the Cadillac?"

Chicka looked doleful. "The Cadillac ran into the Hummer. I told Alf, watch out for that hoon in the Hummer, driving like a maniac. Alf didn't watch out." He sighed. "He never takes my advice."

"So Alf's waiting for the car to be towed?"

Chicka shook his head. "It's drivable. Fact is, Alf got into a blue with the Hummer driver, and then the cops turned up."

"A blue is a fight," I translated for Melodie's benefit.

Eyes wide, she clasped her hands in entreaty. "Chicka! Your brother's been arrested?" I could imagine her as a character witness pleading with a judge for Alf's release.

"Dunno, love. Hope not. Alf's doing his best to talk his way out of it. I got a bit toey with the cops, so Alf told me to come here."

"Toey means excitable," I said to Melodie.

The front door was flung open, and Alf stomped in. "Stone the bloody crows!" he exclaimed. "Did Chicka tell you what happened? That arsehole driving the bloody Hummer deliberately bloody stopped in front of me. Then the cops give me a ticket." He took a deep breath. "Damn-bugger-bitch-bum!"

Chicka bit his lip. "Alf, not in front of the ladies."

"Oh, sorry" said Alf. "But it's bloody maddening. No one knows how to drive in this town."

A quarter of an hour later, calmed by several cups of tea, Alf and Chicka sat in Bob's office as we went over our investigation so far.

"Not Ira Jacobs," said Alf, clearly wounded. "He's a top bloke. You sure he's suss?"

"You sure?" repeated Chicka. "I never saw anything wrong."

"And it's Chicka's area, the financial side," said Alf, "so you'd think he'd notice."

I resisted rolling my eyes.

"Jacobs is more than suspicious," said Bob, "but we'll need an audit, both at the Aussie end and here in L.A. before we can be sure. And remember, Alf, Chicka, you can't act any differently toward him. OK?"

Alf wasn't happy. "All right, we'll try."

Chicka was woebegone about something else. "And Paula Slade's really Tami Eckholdt's sister, put there to spy on us? You sure about that?"

"Absolutely," I said. I trusted Lonnie to get it right.

"Don't breathe a word to Melodie," said Chicka, "but I was dead-set on asking Paula for a date. Suppose that's got the kibosh now."

"Chicka's a sheila magnet," said Alf with a touch of pride.

Chicka and Melodie had raised my eyebrows, but I could see what Chicka might see in her. Chicka and Paula/Patsy! Blimey!

"I almost forgot," said Alf, "but Tami's taken a real liking to you, Kylie. We've got a script conference at Lamb White this afternoon. Tami said if you were free, she'd love to see you."

I had serious misgivings about Tami Eckholdt, but this was another chance to get in with the Lamb White people, so how could I turn it down?

"I'm not tottering around in those high heels again," I said.

Alf looked quite disappointed. "No? You looked bonzer yesterday."

"Have you tried wearing them?" I said. "The really, really high ones? Instruments of torture?"

"I know all about it," said Alf, with a world-weary manner.

Looking at his jumbo brown leather ankle boots, I said, "I very much doubt it."

"Alf's fair dinkum," said Chicka, grinning. "You should have seen him onstage in the chorus line at the Wollegudgerie Footy League Celebration Dinner. He was all got up in green chiffon and high heels. Laugh? I near wet myself!"

CHAPTER FIFTEEN

I was sitting in my office updating my notes on the Hartnidge case when the phone rang. It was Fran, who was manning the front desk, as she usually did when it was Melodie's lunch hour. "Kylie, something's wrong with Melodie."

"What's happened? Is she sick? An accident?"

"No idea," said Fran, who actually sounded concerned. "She just rushed in a minute ago, wearing dark glasses, and went directly to the bathroom. Didn't say hi. Didn't natter on about the audition."

"Nothing about her audition? That sounds serious. Do you mind staying at the front desk while I see what's up?" After Fran had assured me, with requisite sarcasm, that there was no place she'd rather be, I went off to locate Melodie.

Because our offices were in a converted house, the staff bathroom was just that—a bathroom with bath, shower recess, and toilet. I found Harriet outside the door, jigging up and down.

"Kylie," she said. "Thank God! You know what pregnancy does to your bladder? I've got to go, right now, but Melodie won't open the door."

"Use my bathroom. Meanwhile, I'll see if I can extract her from this one." I knocked gently on the door. "Melodie?"

I could make out someone inside wailing, "Go away."

"I'm not going away." I tried the handle. Locked, of course. "Melodie, open this door."

"I can't."

Good thing I had excellent hearing. The door was a substantial one, and Melodie's voice was faint. "You mean the door's jammed? Are you saying you want a locksmith?"

"No locksmith!" This was followed by loud sobs.

"Melodie, open this door, or I'll break it down."

"You wouldn't."

"I would!"

A pause was followed by the sound of the door being unlocked. I went in, closely followed by Julia Roberts, who'd been attracted by the commotion. Melodie plunked herself on the edge of the bath and buried her face in her hands. Sobs shook her slender body. Julia Roberts gave me a look that clearly said, *It's your problem*, before walking gracefully out of the bathroom.

"What the hell's the matter?" inquired Lonnie, putting his head around the edge of the door.

"If you want a bathroom, use mine." I sat beside Melodie and gave her a few comforting pats on the back. "There, there."

Lonnie came all the way into the room. Bending down to look closely at Melodie's hunched form, he said, "What happened? You blew the Refulgent callback?"

Melodie raised her head. I was ashamed to find myself relieved to discover that when Melodie sobbed, her skin became blotchy and her eyes got pinkish-red. Up to now I'd suspected I was the only one in L.A. who looked a wreck after crying. Not that I ever cried...

"I did *not* blow the Refulgent callback." Melodie was very indignant. "I'll have you know I've been cast in the Refulgent commercial. If you don't believe me, ask Larry, my agent."

"Then why all this weeping and wailing?" Lonnie asked.

Melodie bowed her head. "I didn't get the speaking part I was hoping for."

Lonnie put his hands on his plump hips. "You're telling me you're just an extra on the set?"

"An extra?" outraged, Melodie leapt to her feet. "I'm *not* just an extra. If you must know, Lonnie, I have an important role. I follow Beach Refulgent Girl and Amusement Park Refulgent Girl. I'm Laundry Refulgent Girl."

"But no dialogue."

"Will you shut up about the dialogue! It's not an easy role. I'm in this Laundromat, you see, and I have to wink at this good-looking guy, then toss back my head with a laugh"—she paused to give a pale shadow of the tinkling laugh she'd been perfecting for weeks—"and then I smile a Refulgent smile."

"But no actual dialogue?" said Lonnie.

I had to physically restrain Melodie, or I suspect there would have been blood on the floor.

* * *

Denting the pink convertible Cadillac had depressed Alf mightily. He drove the car with only a trace of his former verve. "I'll be returning this damaged beauty to the rental place," he said. "For L.A. I need something tougher. Maybe a Hummer. What do you think, Chicka?"

Chicka wasn't for the Hummer. "How about a truck with a decent bullbar? That'd give you a fighting chance in the traffic around here."

Trucks seemed to be a favorite subject in the Hartnidge family. For the next twenty minutes I heard just about every possible comment one could make about a truck and its equipment. I let my mind drift, contemplating an interesting thought that had occurred to me. Although the Hartnidge twins were virtually indistinguishable, and dressed pretty close to identically, I'd always known who was Alf and who was Chicka. I'd never mixed them up.

"Who was born first?" I asked.

They broke off their truck talk to look at me. "I'm the eldest," said Alf. "Can't you tell? Chicka here's my baby brother."

"Only by ten minutes," he said.

"Being the firstborn changes you," Alf declared.

Chicka muttered something that sounded like, "And not for the better," but fortunately at that point our destination came into view.

The arch over the driveway into Lamb White's studios had the words LAMB WHITE: MOVIES OF INTEGRITY in scintillating blue letters on a silver background. The guards at the gate had the same words on their uniform jackets.

Each of us had to produce proof of identity. Our names were then checked off a list, and we were given visitor badges to wear. Our vehicle was searched. One guard shook his head over the state of the Cadillac's grille.

"A bloody Hummer, mate," said Alf in explanation. "A bloody Hummer."

"Backed into you, did it?"

"No, mate," said Alf. "The Hummer cut me off. Believe me, I've got reflexes like a tiger, but I still couldn't stop in time. Whacked right into the big bastard."

There was much head-shaking all round, then finally we were waved through.

The exclamation queen, Rachelle, was sitting at the reception desk, her curly black hair pulled back in a ponytail, and her notable cleavage hidden by a demure blue outfit that proclaimed LAMB WHITE: WE CARE SO MUCH across her left breast.

Rachelle flashed a professional smile our way, then did a double take, obviously recalling us from the barbecue. "Don't tell me! I know you! The twins! And you!"

"Kylie."

"And you, Kylie!"

A mousy woman in the same blue outfit, but bearing the words LAMB WHITE: PURITY IN FILM, escorted us to a lift and took us up the executive suites. The script meeting was to be held in a conference room, and Tami Eckholdt was waiting outside. Her short copper hair seemed to have an even more metallic sheen than previously, and her tight green dress displayed her impressively fit body to advantage.

She gave a perfunctory greeting to Alf and Chicka but turned her full charm on me. "Kylie, so truly wonderful you could spare the time." She seized my hand in a tight grasp.

"Pleased to be here, Tami."

I reclaimed my fingers with difficulty. Tami gave me the once-over, and said, "You're looking very fit, Kylie. Do you work out?"

"Not so you'd notice."

"I do, myself. Regularly, every day. Lamb White has an executive gym. A healthy mind in a healthy body, you know."

"Interesting," I said.

"It *is*. Perhaps you'd like to come by someday?"

"Maybe someday," I said vaguely.

"Unarmed combat," said Tami.

I stared at her. "I beg your pardon?"

"Unarmed combat. It's a wonderful way to sharpen reflexes, improve balance, and energize one's self-image."

"I'll take your word for it."

Tami laughed as if I'd said something funny. "Oh, you Aussies!" she said. "I just love you to pieces!"

"I suppose we'd better join the others," I said, making moves in the direction of the conference room.

"Later, then, Kylie. Let's talk."

The conference room was over-the-top luxurious. The pale carpet was practically ankle deep; the walls were hung with what had to be original paintings; and the large, round conference table and accompanying chairs were sleekly expensive. Each leather place mat had a bound copy of the Oz Mob script precisely centered. Everyone was provided with a crystal water flask and a crystal glass. One side of the room contained a miniature kitchen setup with an espresso machine and a glass-fronted refrigerator containing a wide selection of fruit juices and other bottled drinks.

My skin prickled with alarm. I'd caught sight of a bloke already sitting at the conference table. Quip. He could blow my cover in ten seconds flat.

While Tami was barking commands at some underling—I noted she had a much harsher tone when speaking to staff—I sidled up to Quip. "You don't know me," I hissed out of the corner of my mouth. "We've never met."

Quip grinned at me. "Why, hello," he said loudly. "I don't believe we've met." He got to his feet to shake my hand. "I'm Quip. Quip Trent."

"Kylie."

He grinned. "Lovely name. Australian, is it?"

"Shall we begin?" Tami asked. It wasn't a question.

There were seven of us—Alf, Chicka, Quip, Tami Eckholdt, and two young men, who stood back waiting, watching Tami like well-trained servants ready to leap to her command. One was dark and one was fair, but otherwise they seemed interchangeable.

"Tami's yes-men," whispered Alf with the closest thing to a sneer I'd ever seen on his face.

"Please note," said Tami, smiling at me, "the egalitarian round-table arrangement. This reflects Lamb White's charter: 'All for one and one for all'."

"I think that's the motto of the Three Musketeers," I said.

Tami frowned. "I don't believe so. If these musketeers are using Lamb White's slogan, there'll be legal action, I'm afraid. We're very zealous in protecting our intellectual property."

Alf suddenly seemed to remember I was supposed to be his girlfriend, putting an arm around my waist and squeezing me till I yelped. "Sorry, love. Come and sit down by me."

"There's a chair here, Kylie," said Tami, "beside me."

Crikey, I was getting popular. They'd be fighting over me next. I ended up with Alf to my right and Tami to my left. Chicka sat on Tami's other side, and next to him was one of the nameless yes-men. The circle was completed by the other yes-man next to Alf, and Quip beside him.

Tami looked around the table with a complacent air. I had the sense she particularly liked meetings where she was in charge. "For those of you who don't know him, let me introduce Quip Trent, an experienced script doctor," Tami said. Quip nodded modestly.

Experienced? I happened to know Quip had written several screenplays but had never had one picked up.

Chicka, perturbed, cracked his knuckles. Alf glared at him. Tami looked pained.

"Why do we need a script doctor?" Chicka asked. "The thing's been rewritten by your people at least six times. Hardly anything's left of Vinnie Morgan's Aussie script, and I thought it was crash-hot."

Alf said warningly, "Chicka, mate. Tami knows what she's talking about. She's the expert here, and don't you forget it."

"I still don't think we need all these bloody rewrites."

Tami appeared to make a real attempt to appear patient, but the challenge was too much for her. "For an amateur it may seem strange, but it's the process we use here in the industry, Chicka," she said in an icy tone. "Many writers contribute, each adding his or her own take on the project. Then, if necessary—and it *is* necessary here—a script doctor comes in to smooth any rough edges before the final rewrite. And, of course, the director will be making ongoing changes during the shoot."

"Shit!" said Chicka inelegantly. "You lot will rewrite the bloody thing to death." I couldn't remember ever hearing Chicka swear.

"Thank you for your contribution, Chicka. Now, if we can move on, there seems to be a general agreement the story arc is sagging a little in the second act."

"What do you mean?" Alf asked. "There's lots happening between Penny Platypus and Kelvin Kookaburra."

"There's no real emotional connection between these characters," said Tami. "We need something to fully engage the children in our primary audience." Her yes-men murmured agreement.

"Kids like little things," I said. "How about baby animals?"

"Baby animals are good," said Tami, beaming at me approvingly.

"Let's see," I said. "If a wombat and a bandicoot had a child, that'd be a womcoot, or a bandiwom. And how about a kangaroo and a platypus falling in love? They'd have little platkangs, or maybe kangaplats." I was just warming up. "And there could be kookawallas—"

"Aaagh!" Tami's face was contorted with horror. "No Lamb White movie has interspecies relationships!"

"What? They can't be friends?" Alf protested. "That's the whole point of the Oz Mob."

"They can be *friends*," snapped Tami, "but no sex. Absolutely no hint of mating. The whole topic is absolutely forbidden."

Disgust contorted her face. "The very thought of a kangaroo and platypus falling in love…" She gagged.

"You're right," I said, "the size differential's too great, plus Penny Platypus would be spending most of her life in water. I'm afraid the relationship's doomed before it begins."

Tami's face now reflected suspicion. Could she actually have the rudiments of a sense of humor and realize I was having fun with her?

"This subject is closed," she said. Her yes-men nodded. "Now, to move to the next item, I have a problem with Kelvin Kookaburra. His dialogue seems a little…how shall I put it? Homosexual." Deep disgust had returned to her face.

"Oh?" said Quip, frowning. "Could you point out an example of this, Tami?"

Tami picked up her copy of the script and flipped pages noisily. "Page twenty has Kelvin speaking with Penny Platypus." Her mouth twisted with distaste. Tami was certainly asking a lot of her facial muscles this afternoon.

Everyone obediently flipped pages to find the place. Tami put on red-framed reading glasses. "Quoting Kelvin's words, the script has him saying to Penny Platypus the following: 'Omigod, Pennicles, where did you get that divine outfit? Isn't it just darling!'"

She put down the script and looked accusingly around the table. "Is it just me, or is that a gay kookaburra talking?"

"I think it's just you," said Quip cheerfully.

"Sounds gay to me," said one of the yes-men. The other one nodded emphatically.

"Maybe Kelvin is just a touch effeminate," I said.

Tami frowned heavily. "Lamb White movies always portray genders as very distinct. We see it as our God-given duty to present malleable little minds with role models of real men and real women. Effeminacy is *out*."

"So," said Quip, busily scribbling notes. "You're asking for an ultrabutch kookaburra." He gave her a sly smile. "Have I got that straight?"

I repressed a grin.

Any impulse to smile rapidly disappeared when I realized Tami's knee was pressing against mine. I moved fractionally. Tami's knee followed. I glanced at her. She sent me a meaningful little smile.

Hell's bells! I was a victim of sexual harassment. Sexual harassment from a sheila who specialized in unarmed combat. Wouldn't it rot your socks!

CHAPTER SIXTEEN

The script meeting was coming to an end, which was fine by me. I'd managed to move my chair so I was out of reach of Tami's questing knee, but every now and then she unnerved me with a flirtatious glance.

While everyone argued over plot points in the script, I rehearsed several imaginary conversations with Tami. In each I explained kindly but firmly why I wasn't available for hanky-panky. A polite thanks-but-no-thanks approach. Unfortunately, the fact that I was supposedly Alf's girlfriend hadn't dissuaded her, which was a worry. Maybe I'd have to get tough.

Getting tough reminded me of Tami's devotion to unarmed combat. Sure, I'd done a course in self-defense at the Wollegudgerie Police Club, but I had to be realistic. It was doubtful I'd be able to handle a Tami Eckholdt frontal assault. I shuddered at the disturbing vision of Tami pinning me down with some mysterious unarmed-combat hold, and—

"You OK, love?"

"Thanks, Alf. I'm fine."

To banish such horrible images, I forced myself to concentrate on the meeting. Tami was declaring forcefully there was no way Kelvin Kookaburra, as portrayed in this script, would have the moxie to challenge the evil Gordon Goanna in the climactic scene.

"What's this moxie you're talking about?" Alf asked. "Is it something to do with Kelvin's muscles? Kookas are heavy-duty birds, not pushovers like sparrows."

I was also keen to hear what moxie might be, but Tami had no opportunity to answer, as the focal point of the conference room shifted dramatically. Brother Owen swept through the door, closely followed by a bloke in a pinstripe suit.

The yes-men scrambled to their feet. Tami's expression switched from peeved to welcoming yet deferential. "Brother Owen! This is an honor."

Brother Owen had a faint, smug smile on his smooth, fleshy face. He put up his right hand in benediction. "Blessings upon this meeting, and upon each child of God present with us here."

I was puzzling over this, wondering if Brother Owen meant that one or more of us was *not* a child of God, so it was a selective blessing, when Alf said to the other bloke, "G'day, Marty-O. Long time no see."

So this was the Hartnidges' famous Hollywood agent, Marty O. Ziema. He was average height and very nattily dressed in a blue, double-breasted pinstripe suit, white shirt, and blood-red bow tie. He had gold cuff links, two heavy gold rings, and I caught a flash of gold in one front tooth. I couldn't see it, but I'd take bets his watch would be a heavy gold number.

I recalled Quip describing Marty O. Ziema as ruthless, egotistical, and dishonest—qualities that had made him very successful. "When you've got influence, you have power," Quip had said. "And when you have power in this town, you can do what you damn well please."

I'd imagined a shifty-eyed creature with rat-like features, probably chewing a cigar. Marty-O, however, had no cigar and appeared quite boringly normal, except for the bow tie. Mum always said to watch out for blokes wearing bow ties. "They're a bit off," she'd say. "Not quite your ordinary bloke." Now that I looked at him closely, his eyes were rather beady and close together.

Alf got up to shake Marty-O's hand. "I was just saying to Chicka—when was it, Chicka, yesterday morning?—where the hell's Marty-O got to? Didn't you get our messages?"

"Messages?" said Marty-O. "You left messages?"

A line from my *Complete Handbook* popped into my head: *Liars often repeat questions; it's a stalling mechanism, while the person fabricates an answer.*

"We did," said Chicka. "You were always in a meeting, or out of town."

Marty-O's face suddenly transformed from bland to twisted rage. "My fucking assistant's fucked up for the last time. I'll fire the bitch."

Alf looked horrified. "Holy cow, I don't want to get anyone fired."

"Alf," said Marty-O, abruptly becoming calm and very serious, "when one of my clients, one of my *major* clients, has anything less than the absolute ultimate in unsurpassed service, someone has to pay. Pay dearly." He shook his head ruefully. "I mean, Alf, ask yourself, where would Marty-O be in this town if he didn't promptly return every call?"

One of the yes-men sniggered. A burning glare from Tami sobered him quick smart.

"My friends!" boomed Brother Owen in his deep, resonant voice. Apparently the attention had been off him for long enough. When he had everyone looking his way, he went on, "I am here with a purpose." He flicked a glance at Tami. "Your meeting has concluded?"

"Yes. Yes, it has, Brother Owen."

"Excellent." He indicated Tami's yes-men and Quip. "You may leave us." Then his gaze stopped at me. "Kylie, how delightful to see you again."

I was impressed he'd remembered my name. "Bonzer to see you too."

"I've been wanting to speak with you about something. Something important."

"You have?" I said, astonished. To him I was just Alf's Aussie girlfriend, so what could he want with me?"

Quip, who'd gathered up his things and was following the yes-men out of the room, raised an eyebrow in my direction, and mouthed, "Lucky girl."

When the three men had left, closing the door behind them, Brother Owen said to the agent, "Marty-O, if you wouldn't mind, I'd like a glass of mango juice with ice." He gestured toward the refrigerated glass-fronted cabinet.

Marty-O stared at him. "You want *me* to get you a drink?" He indicated Tami, and then me. "Surely..." His expression made it clear he considered this was women's work.

Brother Owen appeared surprised to have any discussion on the matter. "And while you're there, Marty-O, I'm sure others would like some refreshments too."

Marty-O hesitated, then, face red and lips compressed, he went over to the mini kitchen. I had to bite the inside of my cheek to prevent myself from grinning. Brother Owen was quite an operator. In the clash of titanic egos, it was Brother Owen one, Marty-O nil.

I wandered over to get my own orange juice. Marty-O glanced my way but didn't speak. "G'day," I said. "I'm Kylie." He ignored me.

Brother Owen indicated we should take our seats around the table. "Before we begin, I have an invitation for you all. This Saturday evening the Church of Possibilities will be holding our famed annual fund-raising gala for children stricken with cancer. This exclusive, star-studded event will be attended by the cream of Los Angeles society. As you might imagine, although very expensive, tickets are snapped up months before the gala, leaving many disappointed socialites and other, lesser people."

"One of the events of the year," said Tami.

"Not one of the events, Tami. *The* premier event of the Los Angeles charity social calendar." He spread his arms wide. "And

I'm extending to each of you an invitation to be my guest at the central table of honor."

"We'll be there," said Alf.

Chicka nodded enthusiastically. "Anything to help the sick kiddies."

"Excellent." Brother Owen turned to me. "And you, my dear? I hope you're free?"

Thank heavens I had the perfect excuse to dip out. "It's a blow, but I'm not free, I'm afraid. My aunt has just flown in from Australia."

"Your aunt? Bring her along." Brother Owen smiled expansively. "I imagine she'll be thrilled to rub shoulders with the many celebrities attending the gala."

"I'll ask Aunt Millie, but I can't promise anything."

Brother Owen switched his attention to Alf. "I'm counting on you to bring Kylie and her Aunt Millie to the gala."

Dismay clouded Alf's features. I knew he'd do almost anything to avoid seeing Millie. "I dunno…"

"Thank you, Alf. I knew I could rely on you. Everyone, Tami will be advising you later regarding tickets, parking, and security procedures at the gala. Now, before we continue further, let us pray for guidance."

Clasping his hands on the table in front of him, he bowed his head and waited until the coughs and foot-shufflings had ceased.

"Guiding Spirit," Brother Owen began, using that singsong addressing-the-heavens tone I'd noticed preachers often favored, "in the darkness of the night you spoke to me, enlightened me. You revealed a revelation. 'Brother Owen,' you said, 'your vision of your role in the Church of Possibilities is too small, too limited, even though, according to the latest available figures, it is one of the most successful ministries in the world.'"

During the pause that followed, I opened my eyes. I reckoned the Guiding Spirit would know everything as a matter of course, but I had to admit I was surprised it seemed necessary to put in a mini-ad for COP while in the middle of a revelation.

Sneaking a quick look at the others, I found everyone but me had their eyes shut, except for Marty-O. He was glaring at a point on the table top so fiercely I found myself checking to see if he'd melted a hole.

"Guiding Spirit!" We were off again. I shut my eyes. "I am the leader of an immense and ever-growing flock, each person yearning to reach their God-given potential. Even as leader, it is humbling to find I, too, can be shaken with negative thoughts of uncertainty and indecision."

Another pause. "Yet at that murky moment—the dark night of my soul, if you will—your voice spoke to me, yet again. 'Brother Owen,' you said. 'Hark.' And I harked. Then came those inspiring, transcendental words: 'If Mel can do it, so can you, Brother Owen.' "

"Who's Mel?" I heard Chicka whisper.

"Not now!" Alf hissed.

Brother Owen was building to a crescendo. "Guiding Spirit! I accept this great task you have entrusted to me, and will bring it to full, glorious fruition. Amen!"

Sitting back with a satisfied sigh, he said, "So? What do you think?"

No one spoke. Chicka looked mystified. Alf was bewildered. Marty-O examined his fingernails.

"Could we have more details of the great task?" I said.

"Of course you may. The moment I had this revelation, and realized the Oz Mob characters were involved, I contacted Marty O. Ziema to discuss the concept in depth. Tell them, Marty-O."

Marty-O didn't look too happy. I reckoned he wasn't used to being treated like the hired help. He cleared his throat. "Brother Owen believes his life story is—"

"Not believes. *Knows.*"

"Brother Owen knows his life story is the stuff of legend." Marty-O's voice had an irritating mosquito whine to it. "Religion is big at the box office. Religious books are at the top of best-seller lists. In these trying times, audiences are craving the spiritual, and to reach them effectively you need—"

"The multigenerational approach!" interrupted Brother Owen. "That was my revelation—to simultaneously reach out to the whole spectrum of humanity. To run the gamut from the very young to the very old, and everyone in between."

"Where's the Oz Mob come in?" asked Chicka, his face suspicious. "You're not trying to dump us, are you?"

Brother Owen appeared deeply offended. "Absolutely not. Let me explain my vision in its entirety, and your unreasonable fears will be laid to rest."

Brother Owen held up on finger. "First, the Brother Owen autobiography. My ghostwriter has almost finished the first draft. I'm calling it *The Radiance of Brother Owen*."

"Catchy title," I said.

He nodded. "I think so." He held up finger number two. "Second, the movie of my life. Tami?"

"It's a wonderful screenplay," said Tami. "Lamb White is throwing every resource into developing this project."

"*I* wrote the screenplay," announced Brother Owen with a proud smile. "The movie will also be called *The Radiance of Brother Owen*."

"Good tie-in," said Marty-O. "And you could have copies of your autobiography for sale at every cinema."

"Excellent idea. Tami, jot that thought down."

"If you wrote the screenplay, why didn't you write your autobiography too?" I wanted to know.

"If only I could have, my dear." He shook his head regretfully. "Every moment to me is so valuable. The screenplay I dashed off in a week or so, but books have so many more words, and I have so little time. A ghostwriter was imperative. Of course, I'll be overseeing every word, every phrase."

"Mate, this is all very interesting," said Alf, "but what about the Oz Mob?"

Brother Owen held up a third finger. "The Oz Mob movie is the third prong in my spiritual assault on the material world."

"We're well along with the Oz Mob screenplay, Brother Owen," said Tami, eager to please. "Our meeting today was particularly productive."

He waved a dismissive hand. "It'll have to be completely rewritten, and the title changed too."

"Rewritten?" said Tami faintly.

"Totally."

"But the concept's the same?"

"Haven't you been listening? The concept's entirely different."

"What's the new title?" demanded Alf.

"The Oz Mob in Eden."

"Evocative title," said Marty-O. "I see a tie-in with picture books. Pop-up ones, with the apple tree and serpent."

"Tami, jot that down."

"I don't get it?" said Chicka, sounding really pissed-off.

"Visualize this!" Brother Owen commanded. "Picture the eager faces of children, as, accompanied by their loving parents, they flock to the cinemas. There they sit in the darkness, their enchanted eyes fixed on the images of those wonderfully cute Oz Mob creatures. Consider the impressionable young brains ready to be subtly imprinted with ways of thinking that will gently lead them, inevitably, to the Church of Possibilities."

Alf and Chicka looked at each other, then at Brother Owen. "Look here," snapped Chicka, clearly very upset. "Five minutes ago Alf and I had a movie, and we had a script—even though it'd been buggered about with something awful. Now you're saying what? It's going to be something else altogether? We've got a signed contract, remember."

With a silky smile, Brother Owen said, "And I would advise you to read the fine print of that contract. You'll find you've given Lamb White the future movie rights to the animal characters. I want to work with you boys, but if you force my hand…"

"Standard practice," said Marty-O quickly. "Good for the Hartnidges. Good for Lamb White."

Obviously unhappy, Alf said, "So what's this new film about?"

"It will be a timeless story of a man named Adam and his God," Brother Owen enthused, "set in an Aussie Garden of Eden populated by adorable little animals."

"What happened to Eve?" I asked.

Brother Owen gave me a tolerant smile. "My dear young woman, being a foreigner, I can't expect you to be familiar with our philosophy. Let me be very clear. No child's eyes will ever see a naked man and woman together on the screen in a Lamb White movie."

CHAPTER SEVENTEEN

"And then," I said to Ariana and Bob Verritt, "Brother Owen assured Alf and Chicka this was just the beginning. After the Garden of Eden, the Oz Mob characters would be starring in a series of biblical movies. There'd be Oz *Mob and the Ten Commandments*, *Moses and the* Oz *Mob*, Oz *Mob and Sodom and Gomorrah*, and—"

"Wait a minute," said Bob. "I thought Lamb White didn't show the naughty bits. Sodom and Gomorrah is loaded with sex. Deviant sex, at that."

I grinned. "Made that last one up," I said. "No one even mentioned Sodom and Gomorrah."

"And how did Alf and Chicka take all this?" Ariana asked.

"Not well at first, but Marty-O painted a rosy picture, telling them the movie budgets would be bigger, the special effects enhanced, the sales of Oz Mob toys astronomical. They were wavering. The turning point came when he said, 'Trust me, I'm your agent.'"

"And they trusted him?" said Bob. "Marty O. Ziema?"

"I'm afraid so."

"Jeez," said Bob.

There was a moment's silence while we all contemplated Alf and Chicka's trusting natures.

"While I'm thinking about it," I said, "Tami criticized Kelvin Kookaburra because he didn't have moxie. What's moxie?"

"Pluck, courage," said Ariana.

"Guts?"

"Guts."

Then I told them about the invitation to the Church of Possibilities charity gala for cancer-stricken kids.

"I'll see you there," said Ariana.

Crikey, and I wasn't aiming to go. "You will? How come?"

"I'm Nanette Poynter's guest. Her husband has no idea I'm a private investigator. I'll be passed off as a dear friend of Nanette's who has just returned to Los Angeles."

"Actually, Ariana, I wasn't planning on attending."

"No?"

"It's because of Aunt Millie."

"Oh, hey, I'll look after her for you," said Bob. "You go ahead and enjoy yourself."

"The fact is," I said, "when Brother Owen heard my Aunt Millie was in town, he invited her to the gala too. I'm not that keen on taking my aunt to something like that. She'll find a zillion things to criticize."

"Simple solution," said Bob. "Don't tell her anything about it. She won't miss what she doesn't know."

"I can't do that," I said. "She's been given an official invite. I have to pass it on."

"So what if she accepts? Then you're in trouble."

"I'll try persuading her it's not her cup of tea." I couldn't stop a sigh. "If Aunt Millie senses I don't want her to do something, she'll do it—she's very contrary."

Ariana grinned. "Another thing that runs in the family."

"Anything else to report?" Bob asked.

"Brother Owen said he had something important to tell me, but he never got around to telling me what it was."

"I'd watch out for those holy types," said Bob. "He'll suck you into his phony church."

"There's nothing else, except the sexual harassment." That got their attention. I described Tami's interest in unarmed combat, and how she'd played kneezies with me under the table. All this amused Bob exceedingly.

"You think it's funny to have a pint-size, mega-fit, metallic-haired sheila make a blatant play for you?" I said heatedly. "Because if you do, Bob, you're dead wrong. It's downright alarming."

"I'd back you any day against the Eckholdt woman," said Bob, still grinning. "Think how much information you could get from her. You could string her along, be a regular Mata Hari."

"Mata Hari came to no good," I pointed out. "She was executed by a French firing squad."

"You know the damnedest things," said Bob.

"If it gets too difficult," said Ariana, "have Alf Hartnidge tell Tami Eckholdt he's broken up with you, and won't be seeing you anymore."

"But then I don't have an in at Lamb White. I suppose it's worth the danger...I hope."

* * *

Fran was packing up for the day when I found her. She'd been on the reception desk most of the afternoon, because, in a gesture I'd never have credited her with, she'd offered to take the broken-hearted Melodie's place so Melodie could go home early.

"You really are terrific, Fran," I said. "It was sweet of you to fill in for Melodie."

She eyed me distrustfully. "You want something?"

"I don't want anything. Well, maybe, yes."

"Ah-ha! I knew it!" Fran was always pleased to have her worst suspicions confirmed.

"Just a little information. I ran into Quip at Lamb White this afternoon. I was surprised to see him."

"Didn't Chicka Hartnidge tell you?"

"Chicka had something to do with Quip being there?"

"I may have mentioned to Melodie that Quip would love to work on the Oz Mob screenplay. And Melodie may have mentioned this to Chicka. And Chicka may have mentioned Quip's name to Tami Eckholdt."

"May have? *Did* you mention it to Melodie?"

"It's the way things work in this town. It's who you know, Kylie. You cultivate the people who can pull strings for you."

"What happened to talent? Doesn't that count anymore?"

Fran narrowed her eyes. "Are you saying Quip isn't talented?" she asked in a menacing tone.

"Of course not, Fran." Her dangerous expression was fading, until I added, "Although, in all honesty, I don't have any way of knowing one way or the other."

"Quip is brilliant," she snarled, eyes down to slits again. "You can take my word for it."

"Right-oh."

"It's purely bad luck he hasn't had any of his screenplays picked up. It'll happen. Soon."

I suddenly wished I had someone who believed in me the way Fran believed in Quip. "I'm sure you're absolutely right. I mean, what would I know?"

"Exactly. What *would* you know?"

Harriet, on her way out, stopped to say good night. "I see Melodie collected her pound of flesh," she said to Fran.

Fran made an indeterminate sound that could have meant anything.

I must have looked puzzled, because Harriet said to me, "You didn't know Melodie got Chicka to persuade Lamb White to hire Quip?"

"I've just heard."

"Of course that means Fran owes Melodie a big favor in return." She grinned at Fran. "Hope it was worth it."

I was disappointed. "So that's how Melodie got to go home early? She called in a favor?"

Fran tossed off a derisive laugh. "You thought I'd do this for Melodie from the goodness of my heart?"

"Well, yes, I did."

"More fool you," said Fran. I thought she looked a bit embarrassed.

Harriet passed the delivery bloke on her way out the front door. He and I didn't get on too well. He was the pushy, too-friendly sort with a nasty streak to go with it.

Dumping several packages on the desk, he said to me, "And how's little Nancy Drew this afternoon?"

Ever since he'd sprung me reading *Private Investigation: The Complete Handbook*, the delivery bloke had given me a hard time.

"Detecting my little heart out," I said. "Thank you for asking."

He grinned knowingly at Fran. Jerking his head in my direction, he said, "Hey, Fran, watch your back. Before you know it, the girl detective here will be running the whole show."

Fran shot me a cold look. Fair dinkum, this woman could hold grudges. "What makes you think she isn't already?" she snapped.

* * *

I was all set to have dinner with Aunt Millie but got a merciful reprieve when she called to say Disneyland had exhausted her so she wanted an early night.

"What did you think of Disneyland?" I dutifully inquired.

"Far too happy," she said. "All that joy and gladness. It's not natural."

"About tomorrow," I said, "Friday's always a busy day for me—"

"Universal."

"Pardon, Aunt Millie?"

"Universal Studios. I'm booked on a tour. I'll see you tomorrow night."

Who would have thought my aunt would take such an interest in the cultural icons of L.A.? I took a deep breath. I had to bite the bullet. "Aunt Millie, you've been invited to a charity gala, but I don't know if you'd be interested. You probably won't be. It's fine if you're not."

"I'll go. When is it?"

I felt myself droop. "But, Aunt, you don't know anything about it."

Aunt Millie snorted. "I imagine you're about to give me all the details. Go on, then." I went on. Aunt Millie asked searching questions. I answered them as best I could.

"This Church of Possibilities," she said, "is it a satanic cult?"

I found myself grinning. "Quite possibly. Even probably."

"Should be an interesting evening." She sounded pleased, which in itself was unsettling.

"I have to admit, Aunt Millie, I'm surprised. I didn't think a charity gala like this would be the sort of thing you'd like."

"That's how little you know about me, Kylie. In my day I was quite wild."

My Aunt Millie?

"Wild? What sort of wild?"

"None of your business, my girl. Now, I need to go shopping for something suitable to wear to this gala affair. You're free on Saturday morning, I presume? Perhaps we could do Rodeo Drive."

"Rodeo Drive!"

"Kylie, do you have any idea how annoying it is to have someone repeat words back to you? I'm afraid it's becoming a habit of yours. I strongly advise you to break it."

* * *

While Julia Roberts consumed tuna for dinner, I sat in the kitchen with a cup of tea and made a list of things to do on the Hartnidge case. I headed it TAKE ACTION! to impress on my subconscious the need to get moving.

It was important to find out what was going on at the Australian end, and to establish if the source of the opals was Ralphie's Opalarium. Lonnie hadn't got back to me yet on whether Ron Udell or Ira Jacobs had traveled to Australia lately, or if Brother Owen had visited Wollegudgerie.

Then there was the Oz Mob office in Burbank. Apart from Jacobs and the creepy Udell, Paula/Patsy was a major suspect, especially as she was the person in charge of shipping the toys into the country.

Alf and Chicka would have to be the ones to organize an audit of their company's books. All I could do was suggest they hurry up and have it carried out, both here and in Oz.

I pondered over the list, putting at the end a note to have one of the Hartnidges fax our office a copy of the contract they'd signed with Lamb White. Harriet would know where to get the best legal opinion on a document like this. I had a strong suspicion the fine print Brother Owen had referred to would contain the key clauses, and they would all be to Lamb White's advantage.

When I'd finished, I read the list to Julia Roberts, who listened with an abstracted air. The squirrels were having a party on the roof tonight, and at least one appeared to have invested in lead boots. At least, I hoped they were squirrels. Lonnie had given me hair-raising stories about L.A. tree rats. He claimed they lived in palm trees, were big as cats, and most had rabies.

Naturally I'd asked if Lonnie had ever seen one of these monstrous rats. He'd been forced to admit he hadn't, not personally, but he knew a woman who had. Indeed, Lonnie assured me, her miniature dachshund had almost been whisked away by a pack of the colossal rodents and was only saved when she heard its cries of distress. I'd demanded the person's name and number. Lonnie became evasive. Perhaps it was a friend of a friend…

There was another scuffle on the tiles above us. "Would you protect me from a rabid tree rat, Jules?"

She washed her face, spending special time on her whiskers. I guessed the answer was a qualified no. You could never tell with Julia Roberts. She'd put herself on the line for me once before, so why not do it again?

I checked the time. It would be Friday morning in Wollegudgerie. One item on my list was to check with Bluey Bates. I could do that right now. I dialed his number.

"Kylie, love. How's things?"

He sounded so subdued, I said, "What's the matter, Bluey? And don't say 'nothing.' I can tell there's something wrong."

"I was going to ring you darl, really I was, but..."

"Is it about Ralphie?"

"Yeah." Our voices were traveling across the wide Pacific Ocean, but Bluey's sigh was as clear as if he'd been in the room with me.

"The stolen opals?"

"Yeah. He as good as admitted to me he was in on it, but I said to him, 'Don't tell me, Ralphie, or I'll have to do something about it,' so he shut up."

"Is there anything you can let me know?"

"One thing. Ralphie's not the brains in the family by a long shot. He isn't smart enough to set this up himself. Someone approached him with a deal. He was to get a percentage of the proceeds, but I don't believe he's seen any money yet."

"Any idea who set it up?"

"If it had been anyone local, Kylie, word would have got around. You know what the 'Gudge is like. I reckon most people are pretty sure Ralphie had something to do with the robbery, but no one's said anything to me. And Mucka Onslow doesn't have a clue, as usual."

"So you're thinking someone pretending to be a tourist lobbed in and contacted Ralphie?"

"Funny thing," said Bluey, "the week before the opals disappeared, I ran into Ralphie in the company of a couple of Yanks. I would have stopped for a chat, but my brother couldn't get rid of me fast enough."

I sat up straight. "Did you get their names?"

"I didn't, but I know they were staying at the Wombat's Retreat."

This wasn't surprising. Except for a few bed-and-breakfasts, Mum's pub was the only accommodation in town. Bluey worked out the approximate date he'd seen the blokes with Ralphie, and I said I'd check direct with Mum.

"Ralphie's such a bloody fool," said Bluey. "But he's family, so I have to stick by him. Thank God our mum and dad aren't here to see him behind bars. That's where the stupid bastard's going to end up, you know."

What could I say? Poor Bluey was absolutely right.

I said goodbye and hung up, then picked up the phone to call Mum. I hesitated. Coward that I was, I didn't want to say to her, "Don't keep asking me to come back to help you run the Wombat. It's not going to happen." She'd be upset, and probably cry, and I'd feel awful.

Still, this was business. This was my first real case. I punched in the numbers briskly, before I could change my mind.

Mum was distracted. "Kylie, lovely to hear from you dear, but I'm waiting for the plumber. The hot water's off, and wouldn't you know it, we've got a full house."

I told her the information I wanted. "Do you mind, dear? I'll put Rosie on. She can look it up for you."

"Who's Rosie?"

"She's new. Not great, but she'll have to do for the moment. Since you've been gone, I've had trouble coping with the paperwork. Millie will tell you all about it."

Fortunately, before Mum could really get going on this subject, the plumber turned up, and I was transferred to Rosie. Rosie didn't seem too bright, and it took her ages to find the registration details I wanted, but I finally heard one name I recognized.

I would have never thought the security procedures brought about by rising terrorism in the world would ever be of help to me, but I was wrong. Everyone registering in the Wombat's Retreat had to provide identification, and foreigners were required to show their passports. Ron Udell, accompanied by a man I didn't know, Simon Wardley, had stayed at the pub the week before the Opalarium burglary.

I thanked Rosie with so much enthusiasm I startled her, hung up, and did a little jig around the room. Who could I call and say how clever I'd been? Then I gave myself a mental slap. I was a professional. I'd wait until tomorrow and coolly mention it to Bob and Ariana.

Thinking of Friday reminded me of my date with Chantelle. We'd had plans to visit a new lesbian bar in West Hollywood on Friday evening, but now Aunt Millie was expecting me to have dinner with her. I called Chantelle to explain the problem.

"Why don't we three have dinner?" said Chantelle. "I'm dying to meet your aunt, having heard so much about her."

"I don't think that's a very good idea."

"And then," said Chantelle, "we can take her along to the bar with us. Show her a bit of the West Hollywood night life."

I gasped. "Take my Aunt Millie to a lesbian bar!"

"Why? What's the problem? Is she narrow-minded?"

"I don't think it's a very good idea."

"You said that before. How about I just ask her when we meet? Leave it for your aunt to decide if she wants to come with us or not."

"Chantelle, you can't ask my Aunt Millie to a lesbian bar. She'd feel out of place."

"She'll have plenty of company. You find lots of straight women there. It's curiosity brings them—taking a walk on the wild side."

I stifled a giggle. "When I was talking to Aunt Millie earlier, she did tell me she'd been wild in her day."

"There you go," said Chantelle. "Aunt Millie can relive her youth."

CHAPTER EIGHTEEN

Friday morning I found Melodie in the kitchen reading *Variety* while her bagel toasted. From her cheerful demeanor I saw she had gotten over yesterday's audition trauma.

I glanced over her shoulder. I'd found that *Variety* and *The Hollywood Reporter* were the official newspapers of the entertainment industry and collectively were called the "trades." They both used odd jargon, understood by the in-crowd. I figured as a private eye I'd be having lots to do with entertainment types, so I was learning the language.

So far I'd established that people who "ankled" had actually left a company or a movie cast, and that every reference to "Mouse House" was actually the Walt Disney organization, but some word usage still puzzled me.

"What's 'Laffer Skein Preems' mean?" I asked, pointing to a headline.

"Comedy series has its premiere. It's show biz talk."

"I know that, Melodie."

My tone was a little tart. Having Aunt Millie around was wearing on my nerves. I'd tried to find out how long she intended to stay in Los Angeles, working on the principle that a finite end to the agony would help me cope, but my aunt had been vague, saying she had an open-ended return ticket on Qantas, and she'd leave when she was good and ready.

"Oh, look," said Melodie, on full alert. "There's something here about the Oz Mob."

"Where?"

"Lamb White's making a series of Oz Mob movies!" Melodie turned sparkling eyes to me. "Kylie! I'll be Penny Platypus in a *series*!" She thrust the paper at me, and assumed the stance of one leaning over a microphone. "Fair dinkum, Penny Platypus here. G'day. How yer goin' mate, orright?" She looked at me, pleased. "What do you think of my Australian accent? My voice coach says I've got the ear."

"Needs work." That was an understatement. It was hard to say what Melodie's accent sounded like, but it certainly was nothing like an Aussie.

"You could give me a few pointers, Kylie, so I could fine-tune my accent. Meryl said the Australian accent was one of the most challenging she'd tried." She added with a satisfied smile, "Funny, isn't it, because *I* haven't found it very difficult."

"You're comparing yourself to Meryl Streep?"

"Of course not. Meryl's an established star, near the end of her career. I'm just at the beginning of mine." She snatched *Variety* back from me and read the paragraph again. "It's fate that Chicka and I met. It's like I was meant to interpret Penny Platypus."

"Don't count your platypuses until they're hatched." Crikey, I was in a sour mood this morning. "What I mean is, Melodie, it's just a proposal. Lamb White isn't committed yet."

Melodie was feverishly slapping cream cheese on her bagel. "Tiffany will just *die* when she hears the news," she said, ankling the kitchen with bagel, coffee, and *Variety* under her arm.

I took my tea back to my office. Lonnie came wandering in, for once not eating, to tell me Ron Udell had visited Australia along with Brother Owen. He'd traced Brother Owen's movements with ease, as the leader of the Church of Possibilities was clearly drumming up as much publicity as possible about setting up a branch of COP in Queensland. This made sense. Queensland was a bonzer state, but the place did seem to attract more than its fair share of way-out religions.

Brother Owen had flown into Sydney with Udell, and then they'd apparently separated, with Brother Owen courting the media in the capital cities of Melbourne, Sydney, and Brisbane, and Ron Udell going off on his own. Lonnie hadn't found out where.

I felt quite smug when I told Lonnie I'd done a bit of detecting of my own, and knew the answer to that question.

After Lonnie had wandered back out again, I checked my TAKE ACTION! list, deciding to eliminate two items with one call. First, I needed the contract Alf and Chicka had with Lamb White faxed to our office. Second, I had to persuade the Hartnidges to initiate a full audit of their company in both Australia and here in the States.

I got Alf Hartnidge on the line. "Kylie, love! Marty-O's been chatting with me and Chicka at an early morning brekkie. He's a good bloke, you know. Wants the best for us." He added with a reverent tone, "Did you see we made *Variety* this morning? *Variety*!"

"I read the item, Alf. Now, Marty-O, what's he been saying?"

Alf and Chicka might be big, strapping Aussies, but even I could see that in L.A. they were babes in the wood.

"Marty-O explained how lucky we are that Brother Owen's so keen to use our Oz Mob in those Bible movies. Chicka's still dragging his feet, but I'm gung ho."

"Has Marty-O suggested you sign any new contracts with Lamb White?"

"He's drawing them up as we speak. Says we need to pin Brother Owen down quick smart, before he changes his mind."

The Hartnidges weren't babes in the wood. They were lambs to the slaughter. "Don't sign any contracts, Alf. Not until a lawyer looks them over."

"Why drag a lawyer into it? Marty-O knows what he's doing."

"He certainly does," I said. "That's your problem right there." It took some fast talking, but I finally managed to get Alf to promise neither he nor Chicka would sign any documents without having them checked out. "I'll get Harriet to call you," I said. "She can give you the names of the best entertainment lawyers."

"If you really think it's necessary…"

"I do, Alf." I added, "And Marty-O will respect you for it." A good thing Alf couldn't see my cynical smile.

There was no problem getting Alf to agree to fax over the current contract he and Chicka had with Lamb White. The problem came with the audit. "But, mate, Ira Jacobs will be asking why we want an audit. It's like we don't trust him, isn't it?"

"You *don't* trust him."

"Yeah, but…"

I was beginning to wonder whether Alf might not have some other reason not to offend Jacobs. "Alf, level with me. Do you fancy Ira Jacobs?"

"I might."

"It's not a good idea to let personal feelings get in the way of business matters."

Crikey, I was sounding like my mother. And I was such a hypocrite. If Ariana ever said the word, I'd be in her arms like a shot, business or no business.

"It's not easy being bi," Alf complained. "If you think about it, you get double the temptations everywhere you go. It's bloody hard to say no."

Normally, Alf's sex life would be none of my business, but Ira Jacobs was a different matter. It was my professional duty, I decided, to find out if Alf was sleeping with the enemy. "I can see how Ira could be very enticing," I lied, "but have you resisted temptation so far?"

"Of course," said Alf with a touch of indignation. "I mean, he's staff. But still…" I was alarmed to hear yearning in his voice.

"Could I speak to Chicka, please?"

Chicka was much more resolute than his brother. He agreed a lawyer was an excellent idea and that an audit was essential. "No worries. I'll straighten Alf out. He tends to let people bamboozle him."

The iron had clearly entered Chicka's soul. I started to say, "You sound much more—"

"Tough? I am. Yesterday when we were getting pushed around by that Bible-basher, I said to myself, 'So what's ten bloody minutes?' "

"Pardon?"

"Ten minutes. Alf thinks being ten minutes older makes him top dog. That he can make all the decisions and I'll go along like a good little younger brother. No more!"

"What does Alf say to this?"

"He keeps on looking at me sideways, like he doesn't know what to make of it. I tell you, Kylie, I should have done this long ago. I'm bloody enjoying myself!"

* * *

Harriet said she'd look out for the fax from the Oz Mob offices and would discuss the contract with a lawyer friend who was in the entertainment business. She could also supply the twins with a list of reputable attorneys.

Bob wasn't in yet, so I went direct to Ariana with my news about Ron Udell being in Wollegudgerie the week before the opal heist. I sat in her office talking it over with her and trying not to look too pleased with myself, which was hard, because she told me I'd done well.

She sat across from me, so remote yet so desirable. I was careful not to act in any way other than a junior colleague would when speaking with a senior colleague. There was no way Ariana had any idea what I felt about her. And yet...

With a jolt it occurred to me that if a beginning private eye like me could learn how to detect lying, someone like Ariana should be able to do it without breaking a sweat. Not that we were talking about anything I'd lie about, such as whether I was in love with her. That wasn't a conversation we were likely to have.

But I *was* trying to hide something—the disturbing fact that, as far as she was concerned, I was besotted. Well, maybe not besotted. That was too close to infatuation. What I felt was more profound. I supposed it was love, though not like any love I'd felt before.

"Kylie?"

"Oh, sorry. I was thinking about—" I could hardly say what I was thinking about. "Thinking about things."

There went that elegant eyebrow again. "What things?"

My thoughts shot round in my head like startled chooks. I came up with, "How Alf and Chicka are going to be swindled out of their Oz Mob rights. I reckon that's what's going on with the smuggled opals."

"How do you see the scenario playing out?"

I looked at her mouth. We'd kissed, twice. Three times lucky? Jeez, I had to concentrate. "How do I see the scenario playing out?"

Whoops, I was repeating the question. I made a mental note not to do that again. I hurried to continue, before she noticed. "Harriet's going to have someone look at the fine print in the contract the Hartnidges have with Lamb White, but I'm sure it's the morals clause that's the key. I believe it will go like this: The opals will be discovered, Lamb White will be shocked, just shocked, that the Hartnidge twins are criminals. I'm guessing here, but I wonder if when the morals clause is activated, there isn't an option to take over the project completely. Something like that, to give Lamb White and the Church of Possibilities total control over the Oz Mob characters."

While I was talking, I ran a systems check. Points from the lying chapter scrolled in my head. Was I touching my mouth or nose? Smiling too much? Explaining too much? I'd only skimmed the last part of that particular chapter in my *Complete Handbook*. It covered how liars gave themselves away not so much by what they were saying but how they said it. I wished devoutly I could remember all of the details.

"I think you're right," said Ariana. "But proving it will be difficult."

Bob came in and I gave him a rundown of the situation so far, then I bolted back to my office to check my *Handbook*. It had proved itself a font of essential PI information. It was fate I'd found this particular volume in a bookshop. I grinned. Now I was sounding like Melodie.

Checking the last section of the lying chapter, I noted the characteristics a liar shows when speaking. They included longwinded explanations; using *I*, *me*, and *mine* much less frequently than truth tellers; a lack of contractions, so a liar says *do not* instead of *don't*; and last, because lying takes mental work, the interesting point that liars tend to speak more slowly while their brains race to get their stories straight.

I ran over my conversation with Ariana. I was pretty sure I hadn't fallen into any of these dead giveaways. A sudden thought occurred to me. What if it didn't matter? What if Ariana didn't care what I felt about her?

I told myself I'd just get on with my life and stop obsessing over someone I could never have anything but a business relationship with.

* * *

In the early evening I picked up Chantelle before collecting Aunt Millie at her hotel. As we drove through heavy—what else?—traffic, I said to her, "Do you think I have moxie? Be honest now."

Chantelle laughed. "Honey, you have so much moxie it's running out your ears."

I wasn't altogether sure this was quite what I wanted to hear, but that's what you get when you fish for compliments.

Aunt Millie, Chantelle, and I ended up at Heavenly Hamburger Steakhouse just off Sunset Boulevard. My aunt's choice—she said she wanted a genuine American hamburger, not any of that McDonald's rubbish. When Chantelle foolishly pointed out McDonald's was an American company, Aunt Millie said McDonald's was multinational, and everybody knew what that meant.

I kicked Chantelle under the table before she could ask what it was everybody knew. Years of conversations with Aunt Millie had taught me to be circumspect.

"How was Universal Studios?" I inquired, changing the subject. Another conversational skill Aunt Millie had taught me over the years.

"Interesting enough, although I can't see how anyone can be frightened by the rides. All that screaming and carrying on. Quite uncalled for. And, of course, like Disneyland, the place is totally spoilt by kids running around everywhere, completely unsupervised. Pathetic how parents today refuse to discipline their offspring. A couple of times I was forced to show them how it's done."

"I bet that went down well," remarked Chantelle.

Aunt Millie fixed her with a gimlet look. "I don't do things to be popular, young woman. I do things to be right."

At that point our waiter came by to ask if everything was to our satisfaction. Poor choice of words. He was plainly unprepared for Aunt Millie's answer. The chef appeared, accompanied by the manager. Other patrons watched in fascination as my aunt pointed out shortcomings she'd detected in the service and the food. She was kind enough to add a remark or two about the restaurant's furnishings as well.

I glanced at Chantelle. She was past being astonished. Now she was trying vainly not to giggle.

When the restaurant staff had done their best to make amends, and we were left alone, Chantelle brought up the subject of Claudene's, the new lesbian bar that had just opened.

"You're suggesting I visit a lesbian bar?" asked Aunt Millie.

"It's just an idea," I said. "You'd probably hate it."

Aunt Millie beamed at Chantelle. "Excellent idea, young woman. You're a creative thinker."

"Aunt Millie," I said, "are you sure? You must be tired after your day at Universal Studios. And there's jet lag too."

"Rubbish. I've got more energy than the two of you put together."

So it was that we three came to Claudene's. It was still reasonably early in the evening, and I found a parking spot not too far away. As we walked toward the bar, I tossed up whether to warn my aunt she might see things not commonly in plain view in Wollegudgerie. But what the hell—if she was going to be shocked, so be it.

The bar wasn't yet as crowded as I was sure it would be later on, so, even though the lights were fairly dim, it was possible to see the decor. Claudene's was all black and chrome, with artful touches of dark red along the edge of the bar and on the barstool seats. The black and chrome was repeated in the tables and chairs that ringed the small dance floor, where a few couples were slowly rotating to soft, romantic music. I reckoned the hard beat would start later, when the place filled up, but for the moment you didn't have to shout to be heard.

"I thought you said it was a lesbian bar," said Aunt Millie accusingly. "I see several men over there."

"They're women," said Chantelle.

My aunt peered harder. "They look like men to me." Before I could stop her, she'd set off to investigate.

"I like your aunt," said Chantelle, watching her progress across the room. "She's feisty."

Feisty wasn't a word we use in Australia, but I'd got the meaning down, I thought. "You mean she's sort of pushy and high-spirited?"

Chantelle gave me a grin. "I was thinking more along the lines of aggressive like a pit bull."

Aunt Millie was engaged in spirited conversation on the other side of the room. There was much hand waving, and then my aunt returned to us. "You're right. They're women." She glared across the room at one butch lesbian who, hands on hips, glared right back.

My heart sank, as it often did when I was with my aunt. "What did you say to her?"

"I don't know what you mean."

"That butch lesbian seems upset with you."

Ignoring this, Aunt Millie asked plaintively, "What has someone got to do to get a drink around here?"

"Aunt, you don't drink."

"I'm drinking tonight."

"Don't look now," said Chantelle, "but she's coming over."

I covered my eyes. "My Aunt Millie's going to end up in a fight in a lesbian bar. Now I really can't go home again."

The butch woman had nearly reached us. She was older than I'd thought, and her short, dark hair was streaked with gray. She wore mostly black leather, plus a chain or two for embellishment, and had one of those strong, striking faces that are hard to forget.

"My aunt didn't mean—"

Her eyes on Aunt Millie, she said to me, "Excuse me. I'm not talking to you." She had a hoarse, too-many-cigarettes voice.

Chantelle, bless her, was poised to intervene, when the woman said to Aunt Millie, "May I have the pleasure of this dance?"

The evening went off well. Chantelle enjoyed herself, Aunt Millie certainly did, and I was fine, until I had an encounter that convinced me Aunt Millie's philosophy (if something bad can happen, it will) had something to it.

I was chatting with Chantelle at the bar while Aunt Millie was dancing up a storm on the floor, when something made me look toward the door. I clutched Chantelle's arm. "Leaping lizards! That's Tami Eckholdt!"

"Who?"

"She mustn't see me."

"Too late," said Chantelle. "She's making a beeline for you. Just who is this woman?"

Tami was bubbling with delight. "Kylie! I didn't expect to see you here!" Her brief gold lame shorts and strapless black top displayed her muscular body to advantage. She seemed a little unsteady on her feet. Drugs? Alcohol? Or, dreadful thought, enthusiasm for my conquest? Yerks!

Tami's expression hardened as she took in Chantelle, who, bless her, was leaning against me with a possessive hand on my shoulder. "And this is…?"

"My girlfriend, Chantelle," I said, with a strong emphasis on *girlfriend.* "Alf knows," I added hastily. "He understands."

"Alf?" said Chantelle.

"I'll explain later," I said.

Alarmingly, a speculative smile had appeared on Tami's face. "I wouldn't have pegged him for a three-way kind of guy, but hey! Why not?"

As Tami was short, I was able to look hopefully over her head. "Surely you're not alone tonight, Tami?"

"I've come alone, but I don't intend to *leave* alone," said Tami, raising goose bumps on my skin as she stroked my arm.

"Hands off," said Chantelle.

Tami bounced on her toes, sizing up Chantelle. I had a horrifying vision of Tami seizing Chantelle and tossing her over the bar. The mirror would break, bottles would shatter, all in slow motion, in the appropriate movie fashion. It was my duty to shield Chantelle with my body. Surely Tami wouldn't throw *me* over the bar. That would be no way to win my love. *Love!* I shuddered.

"Later, sweetheart," Tami said, I'm not sure to which one of us. "I'll see you later."

"Where did *she* come from?" Chantelle asked, watching Tami swagger toward a knot of women at the other end of the bar. "She looks familiar. Is she in the industry?"

"Lamb White."

"Lamb White! She's a lesbian!"

"In the closet. Deep."

Chantelle nodded slowly. "I guess."

I was praying Tami would hook up with someone much more promising than me and wouldn't notice as Chantelle, Aunt Millie, and I slipped away. Fat chance.

"You're leaving?" she said, materializing by my side.

"It appears so."

Tami raked Chantelle with a contemptuous glance. "I'll see you tomorrow, when you're not otherwise engaged."

"Tomorrow?" I said faintly.

"At the gala dinner. I've arranged it so we'll be sitting together." Meaningful smile. "Until then…"

CHAPTER NINETEEN

On Saturday morning I called Aunt Millie, hoping her strenuous time at Claudene's would have dampened her enthusiasm for shopping. No such luck. I was to pick her up and take her to Beverly Hills immediately.

Shopping with Aunt Millie was a life challenge that up to this point I'd been able to avoid, so I wasn't quite prepared for the experience. I soon found nothing much was required of me, other than to follow in Aunt Millie's wake.

She shopped like a small tank, mowing down obsequious or haughty salespeople alike. We did Rodeo Drive, up one side and down the other. Aunt Millie proclaimed it, "Unbelievably overrated!"

Then we moved on to the Wilshire Boulevard department stores. Here Aunt Millie fell in love with Neiman Marcus. We had a light lunch in their restaurant, then my aunt hit the evening wear department.

"May ah help Modom?"

Aunt Millie gazed suspiciously at the superthin saleswoman. "Modom?"

"Yairs. May ah help Modom?"

Aunt Millie gave a cackle of laughter. "I don't know about Modom, but you can help me."

"Yairs," said the saleswoman, not at all amused.

My feet were hurting and my temper fraying, when, praise be, my aunt found an outfit she deemed satisfactory. It was red and sparkly, with a scoop neckline and a sort of floating train affair.

"It's made for Modom," breathed the saleswoman, clasping her hands in counterfeit joy. "The color suits Modom so."

If you'd asked me to pick something absolutely unsuitable for my aunt, this would have been it. However, Aunt Millie was smitten, and only staggered a little when she spied the discreet price tag.

I took Aunt Millie back to her hotel to rest up for the evening and went home to call Alf. When I told him Aunt Millie was definitely coming to the gala, he gave a muffled cry of pain. "She'll be sitting at our table?"

"Of course she will, Alf. She's Brother Owen's guest."

"Kylie, love, please do me a favor. I'm begging you, mate. Begging you. Don't make me chauffeur Millie Haggety to the gala tonight. It's my driving, see. That's the bone of contention between us."

"You had a collision?"

"Not exactly. See, it happened outside the family do at Christmas last. Vehicles everywhere, you understand. The Hartnidges are a big family. I was just parking under a gum tree by the gate, when I somehow ran over Millie Haggety's foot. She should have got out of the way, of course, but she didn't."

"You crushed my aunt's foot?"

Come to think, I dimly remembered hearing something about this but had paid little attention, as to hear her tell it, Aunt Millie's life was a series of near disasters brought about by a malignant fate.

"It wasn't serious," Alf assured me. "Muddy, soft ground. Nothing broken. She only limped for a few months."

"That's a relief. Not permanently crippled then?"

Oblivious to my sarcasm, Alf went on, "But she's holding a grudge against me. Impalpable, she is."

"I think you mean implacable."

"Yeah, that too."

I agreed I'd pick up my aunt and we would all meet at the table of honor at the gala. "Alf, promise me you won't get into a blue with Aunt Millie." I could just imagine the two of them yelling at each other in the middle of the assembled socialite multitude.

"Fair crack of the whip, Kylie! If there's a blue, it'll be Millie Haggety what started it."

* * *

Knowing Ariana was going to be at the gala, I took special care with my appearance. My new hairdo was holding up well, and I chose a simple black dress that was cut to flare a little when I moved. Looking at myself in the full-length mirror I'd attached to the back of my bedroom door, I had to admit I didn't look too bad.

Odds were Ariana would be wearing black too, but as Mum said, it's what you wear with a little black dress that matters. Mum favored wearing a happy face—she claimed that added oomph to any outfit—but as happy faces and Aunt Millie didn't often go together, I settled for opal earrings, and a gold and opal bracelet.

When I got to my aunt's hotel, I called up from the lobby to say I was there to collect her. The place was full of tourists, most wearing shorts and T-shirts, so it wasn't surprising there was a murmur when the lift door opened and my aunt's stout figure swept out arrayed in her new evening dress and sparkling paste diamond drop earrings and necklace.

"See those heads turn?" she said to me.

"I saw, aunt."

She looked at me critically. "You'll never turn heads with what you're wearing, Kylie. Color's what does it. Color and personality."

We arrived at the charity gala for cancer-stricken children a little early, as Aunt Millie hated to be late. I'd carefully mapped out the route in my *Thomas Guide* and was pleased with myself when I drove straight to the Church of Possibilities Cathedral in Culver City. It was hard to miss. Humongous, its gleaming white walls floodlit, it loomed like a feverish view of a maddened architect who'd been given zillions of dollars and told to create a monument to bad taste.

A huge illuminated sign proclaimed: CHURCH OF POSSIBILITIES CATHEDRAL AND CONVENTION CENTER—"OUR PROMISE IS YOUR POTENTIALITY!"

The building had everything—tall imposing columns, golden domes, a wall entirely made of stained glass, lit from within. Rows of fountains spurted water illuminated in changing colors, all garish. Huge angelic statues, some holding swords, others harps, stared down at us mere mortals.

My car was snatched away, and a ticket was shoved in my hand by one of many men in tight white uniforms who were scurrying around opening doors and then whipping vehicles away down into a subterranean area.

A row of stern guards with handheld computers barred the way. Our names were punched in, and we were found worthy to join the ever-thickening parade of guests heading for the main entrance along a wide red carpet. Gems sparkled, teeth sparkled, cries of greeting probably sparkled too. It was a sparkling occasion all round.

"Sparkling occasion," I said to Aunt Millie.

She didn't answer, her attention on the activities of several photographers snapping smiling groups, who'd stop and pose with practiced ease. Each photographer had an assistant who hurried to jot down the names of those photographed in the correct order, left to right. I'd seen photos like these in the social pages.

One of the photographers suddenly popped up in front of us. Aunt Millie grabbed my arm and bared her teeth in a smile more enthusiastic than I'd ever seen before. To the assistant, she said, "Millie Haggety from Australia. Brother Owen's *special* guest. And this is my niece, Kylie."

As the photographer moved on to another group, Aunt Millie said to me, "Wait until they see *this* in Wollegudgerie!"

"It is a bit like the Academy Awards," I observed.

She wasn't listening. "Is that George Clooney over there?"

Before I could stop her, my aunt had rushed into the crowd and disappeared. I hurried after her, now and then catching sight of her sturdy, red-swathed figure.

In the end, she found me. "Where have you been, Kylie? I've been looking for you everywhere."

"You took off after George Clooney."

"Lovely man. We had a nice chat."

We were approaching the entrance to the edifice—the word *building* was hardly worthy of the structure. Two gigantic stone sphinxes guarded the tall, beaten copper doors through which the crowd was streaming.

"Nice," said Aunt Millie. "I like a bit of glam."

I wasn't sure whether she was referring to the building or the crowd around us. I'd thought Aunt Millie's dress rather over-the-top, but it had nothing on the outfits surrounding us. And blonds. There were more blonds than I'd seen in my life. Many were attached to the arms of older men, and all seemed to be laughing and tossing their heads with delight. Could *all* these people be that pleased to be here tonight?

Brother Owen himself led the welcoming committee at the entrance to the ballroom. After the ceremonial greeting, a bevy of young assistants were on hand to lead guests to their tables.

Aunt Millie and I joined the line and waited to be acknowledged by the great man himself. As we got closer, I heard a recorded celestial chorus singing softly. Concentrating, I could just make out the words. The music obviously ran in a continuous loop, repeating endlessly, "Brother Owen! Brother

Owen! All things are possible! Possible! Possible! Only believe. Only believe."

Brother Owen was a smooth operator, indeed. He had every name on his lips, greeting each individual as a close personal friend. We reached the top of the line. "Kylie." Brother Owen smiled into my eyes while massaging my hand. He turned his incandescent smile on my aunt. "And this must be Aunt Millie."

While we'd been waiting, I'd been observing two sleek young men, each holding what seemed to be an electronic organizer. They watched guests approach the top of the line, and one or the other would check the screen they held, then murmur into a lapel microphone. I reckoned Brother Owen had a wireless device in his ear and was being told each name before the person reached him.

The system was efficient. A quick, warm greeting, and then we were passed to a young woman who would guide us to our table.

The banquet room was immense. At one end a broad, shallow stage was floodlit, although at present it was empty, except for a grand piano. I was impressed, in spite of myself, to discover the walls were hung with gigantic tapestries, depicting many separate scenes. Possibly they were biblical, although most figures seemed to be wearing modern dress.

Many round tables filled the area, each glittering with crystal and silver table settings. The room was already crowded, buzzing with conversation, punctuated by bursts of loud laughter.

"Don't like that Owen bloke," said Aunt Millie as we followed the young woman to our table. "Those glib, fast-talking types are all bad news. Watch out for yourself, my girl. He'll be after you like a rat up a drainpipe."

"Thank you for that alluring picture."

"You can laugh all you like. That one's trouble, mark my words."

She halted. "Is that Alf Hartnidge?"

Alf and Chicka were already sitting at the table, but for an instant I didn't recognize them. Both were formally dressed in tuxedos and looked sensational.

"Aunt, I told you he and Chicka would be at our table, remember?"

"I'm leaving it up to you, Kylie, to make sure I don't sit next to either of them. All they talk about is the Hartnidge clan, and a more boring bunch you'd go a long way to find. I'm related to the Hartnidges by marriage, and I've had to endure the family stories for more years than I care to remember."

The woman who'd been guiding us came back to collect us. She had a flat, expressionless face. "You're at Brother Owen's table," she said in tones of awe. "You'll find your place indicated by your name. Brother Owen asks that you not change your place. Each position has been carefully chosen for harmonious vibrations."

Aunt Millie snorted. "Harmonious vibrations, is it?"

Wisely, the young woman didn't engage Aunt Millie in conversation, murmuring, "Blessings," and then hurrying away.

Both Alf and Chicka leapt up as we approached. Alf made an awkward little bow in Aunt Millie's direction. "Millie, you're looking good."

"Not so bad yourself, Alf. Formal wear looks OK on you boys."

I blinked. This was the equivalent of a flowery compliment from anyone else.

"Change the place cards," hissed my aunt out of the corner of her mouth.

"Your wish is my command."

There were ten places at our table. Four names I didn't recognize. Brother Owen had the seat of honor, facing the stage, and a raised high-backed chair, superior to other seating, so I could hardly move his place card. Alf and Chicka were seated to his right and left. I was next to Alf, and then came Tami, who indeed had managed to arrange to sit next to me. Then came the four strange names, with Aunt Millie in the middle of them. I grabbed Tami's place card and switched it with Aunt Millie's. If I had to choose between the two, it'd be Aunt Millie all the way.

The tables around us were filling up fast. A string quartet had appeared on the stage and was vainly attempting to be heard above the sounds of social conversations, which seemed to include the need to shriek people's names upon each first sighting. Waiters appeared with French champagne.

My heart leapt as I caught sight of Ariana. This romantic stuff about seeing someone across a crowded room was right—where she was concerned, I had tunnel vision. She was wearing black, her pale hair swept up in a more elaborate style than usual. As she came closer, I saw her sapphire earrings were almost the same color as her eyes.

Ariana was with Nanette Poynter, who was doing her model-walking routine on the arm of a portly, older guy with a brick-red complexion and only a few strands of remaining hair. He seemed to be on his last legs—I heard him wheezing as he passed by our table on the way to one adjacent. With delight I realized I was positioned so I could see Ariana quite easily. Not that I'd be looking at her, of course…

Ariana had assured me that Nanette Poynter would not acknowledge that she'd ever met me before. The trophy wife of Vernon Poynter was wearing a very tight scarlet dress that showed her ribs and razor-sharp hipbones. She was also bedecked with what I was sure was a fortune in diamonds.

The four people I didn't know arrived at our table and turned out to be two couples, both ancient and both clearly very rich.

Tami Eckholdt still hadn't appeared when Brother Owen made his way to the stage. The noise died down, the lights dimmed in the body of the banquet room, and an even brighter spotlight illuminated him as he raised his hands.

"My friends. The Church of Possibilities is honored, deeply honored, and humble, deeply humble, to have the blessing of your wonderful presences here tonight. You are vibrant examples of the truth, the truth only glimpsed by some, that great success in life is possible. Yet even each of you, in your heart of hearts, must acknowledge that you are still not fully appreciated. You must be aware of God-given talents hidden deep within you that people would marvel at if they only knew."

I saw several people around me unconsciously nodding. Beside me, Aunt Millie hissed, "Load of old codswallop."

Brother Owen began touching hearts with descriptions of children with cancer. I was convinced he was an extraordinary hypocrite but hoped that a fair portion of the money raised tonight would indeed go to help those poor kids.

"She's in my seat!" was whispered fiercely in my ear. Tami was leaning over me, her cheek practically touching mine. "Your aunt is in my seat."

Trying not too obviously to recoil from her, I whispered back, "There's a spare seat over there, between the two couples."

"That's where *she's* supposed to be. Your aunt must have switched the place cards."

"Shhh!" said someone.

With a muffled oath, my thwarted suitor barged around the table and flung herself in the empty chair. "Nasty bit of work," observed Aunt Millie.

Brother Owen, to thunderous applause, finished his speech and came down to take his seat, on the way stopping at several tables for a personal word with a favored few—doubtless those who contributed generously to the church. I noticed Vernon Poynter gained an especially warm response.

Then things followed the same routine as such functions everywhere. There was food, there was drink, there was totally forgettable conversation. I suspected some people were covertly checking their watches and wondering when they could get out of there.

During the main course someone, no doubt famous, played the grand piano, although nobody paid much attention. After dessert and coffee, a turn by a comedian who wasn't very funny, and a truly heartfelt plea by a female oncologist who specialized in treating children with cancer, the real business of the evening began: table-hopping.

I'd been watching Ariana—I couldn't help myself—and had noticed she'd been knocking back the champagne. I didn't drink much at the best of times, so I'd just sipped mine, but every time a waiter offered, Ariana had her glass refilled.

Brother Owen asked Alf to change places with me. When I was seated next to him, he leaned over confidentially. "Kylie, you're a lovely young woman."

"Thank you, Brother Owen." I couldn't resist adding, "It's not to my credit. It's God given, as you, of all people, appreciate."

He looked rather taken aback. "Of course it is, Kylie. The Guiding Spirit's hand is in all creation."

"You wanted to see me about something?"

"I don't know what your employment is at the moment, but I believe we can offer you an excellent package."

"You're offering me a job?"

Brother Owen gave me an indulgent smile as he patted my hand. "We don't offer jobs at the Church of Possibilities. We offer callings."

"You're offering me a calling?"

"It just so happens we have a major campaign to reach the twenty-fives to thirty-fives. The Church is searching for people like you to spearhead our outreach program."

Was this bloke serious? "In the first place, I don't belong to your church," I pointed out. "And for all you know, I could be a devil worshiper."

He patted my hand again. "I can look into your spiritual self," he said, "and see the potential there."

"I'm honored you considered me," I said, with just a hint of sarcasm. "But I'm afraid not."

Not at all put out, Brother Owen pressed a business card into my hand. "Call me," he said.

Tami, who'd been sulking on the other side of the table, was sent off on some task by Brother Owen, so I felt safe enough to get up from my seat and move around. During dinner I'd noticed a faint, dark shadow on Chicka's upper lip.

"Are you growing a mustache?"

Chicka grinned. "Always wanted one, but Alf said no. Now it's a new day dawning." He smoothed the almost nonexistent bristles. "What'd you think? Just a little mustache, or one of those droopy ones?"

"Oh, definitely droopy," I said.

Alf was frowning. "It's a tradition to be clean-shaven in the Hartnidge family."

"What about Uncle Dave?" said Chicka. "He had a beard down to his waist."

"That's different. Black sheep don't count."

The Poynters were socializing at another table, and for the moment, Ariana was alone. I went over to sit beside her. She was playing with the gold signet ring she always wore, turning it round and round on her finger. It was so unusual to see her fiddling with anything. I said, "Is it bothering you?"

She looked down at the ring as though she'd never seen it before. "No." Picking up her glass, she took a sip. The subject of the ring was clearly off limits.

"You've had a lot to drink," I said.

"I have."

"Have you got your car here?"

"No. I came with Nanette and her husband."

"I'll drive you home."

"I'll get a cab."

I looked around. People were beginning to leave. "Ariana, come on. I've got my car here. We'll drop off Aunt Millie and I'll drive you to your door."

She hesitated a long moment, then said, "OK. Thank you."

Tami came back as we were leaving the banquet room. She pressed a business card into my hand. "Call me."

Ariana had said her good nights to the Poynters and walked silently beside me. Aunt Millie bustled along on the other side. A full moon floated in the sky. It seemed an omen.

When my car was brought up, Aunt Millie got in the front and Ariana slid into the backseat. My aunt, who'd obviously enjoyed herself hugely, chatted about the evening. Ariana and I were quiet.

At the hotel, I saw Aunt Millie to her room. As I opened the door, she said, "What's your relationship with Ariana Creeling?"

"We're business partners."

"That's all?"

"Yes, aunt, that's all."

"She watches you."

I stared at her. "What?"

"I noticed how she kept glancing your way tonight. Are you sure the woman isn't keen on you?"

I felt a thrill tingle in my stomach, but I said calmly, "I'm sure, Aunt Millie."

CHAPTER TWENTY

As I walked back to the car, my heart was fluttering. Ariana had moved to the front passenger seat and was staring blankly out the windscreen.

We drove for a while in silence, then she gave a rueful little laugh. "I don't usually have this much to drink. It was stupid of me."

"French champers is hard to resist."

She glanced across at me. "I noticed you didn't drink much."

"It's from working in a pub. It's like being in a chocolate factory. It's everywhere, and you lose interest."

The winding, narrow streets of the Hollywood Hills no longer confused me. Her house was perched on a cliff, overlooking the city. I drove into the area at the back, parked the car, and turned off the engine.

"Thank you," she said, opening her door.

"I'm coming in."

She paused. "There's no need."

"I want to."

Everything hung on one moment of decision. Ariana said, "Gussie will bark, until she recognizes you." Gussie was her gorgeous German shepherd.

Oh, God, I thought, looking at the back of Ariana's neck as she opened the door, *I want to hold you.*

Gussie, once she'd checked me out, was delighted to greet Ariana. She was a beautiful dog, bright and intelligent and handsome, as only a German shepherd can be.

"Shall I take Gussie outside for a few moments? She's been locked in all evening."

She nodded. "Thank you."

When Gussie and I returned, Ariana was just coming out of the bathroom. Her hair was down and she'd washed the makeup off her face. She looked younger, and less formidable, although that might have been a trick of the light.

"Do you want coffee?" I asked.

"I simply want to go to bed."

"So do I."

Ariana looked at me for what seemed a long time. "Kylie, I don't think..." She made a helpless gesture, the first I'd ever seen her make.

I seemed to move through water. It was such a long way to her. And she watched me with her blue, blue eyes. When she shut them, it was as if a light had gone out.

I reached her, halted, thought my heart would burst, thought she'd reject me at this last moment.

But she didn't. I slid into her arms. We kissed, slowly, quite tenderly. I could taste her toothpaste.

I thought then she might draw back, say this was a bad idea, but Ariana was committed, it seemed. She took my trembling fingers and led me into her bedroom.

I'd never seen her bedroom before—I barely saw it now. I was just conscious of wide windows looking out to the lights of Los Angeles spread far below.

We undressed, me with fingers made clumsy with haste, Ariana with assurance, slipping off her clothes with economical grace. Was that how she'd make love? Coolly, competently, never quite involved? I'd take her any way she came. Whatever she wanted to do, I'd do.

Her body was slim and strong and took the breath from me. I watched in a dream as she removed her signet ring and her sapphire earrings and put them in the drawer of the bedside table. Then she flicked off the light. Moonlight flooded the room.

I intended to be gentle, to coax her body into willingness, but it was as though she flipped a switch and in one moment removed all restraint. She was desperate, ravenous, so unlike the Ariana I thought I knew that I was startled, almost shocked.

She was on fire, her skin hot against mine, her need so ferocious that I despaired I could ever meet it. And then I caught her passion like a sweet contagion, and surged to match it. "Ariana!"

"Don't say a word."

We were fused together, our passion molten as the sun. With wild joy I felt her body respond beneath my hands, my mouth. She arched, quivering, on the brink, then plunged into a release that wrenched a long cry from her.

I held her tightly, willing her to say my name, but she turned in my arms and drove every thought from my head except for the raw, insatiable need to have her touch me anywhere, everywhere.

* * *

In the early morning light, I lay beside Ariana gazing into her unguarded face, gentled by sleep. I'd never made love before like this, been so totally consumed by another person. I'd believed I knew what love was. I'd been wrong.

It sounded so trite when put it in words, but I did love Ariana completely—body, mind, and spirit. And I feared I could never risk telling her that I did.

CHAPTER TWENTY-ONE

When she opened her eyes, it was the unruffled, detached Ariana back in control. She said, "Good morning," as though we'd just met in the hallway of the offices, then swung herself out of bed in one graceful movement. She put on a silk dressing gown—not black, for a change, but a pale green—and went into the bathroom. She put her head out to tell me there was a guest bathroom, and where I would find a towel.

I got up, collected my clothes, and went to have a quick shower. I realized with a shock that I didn't want to face her this morning. She'd see in my eyes what I felt about her. And she'd be detached but kind. How I'd hate that.

Examining myself in the bathroom mirror, I found I looked reassuringly normal. I tried a smile. Not a success. This was going to be hard.

When I opened the bathroom door, Gussie came in, wagging her tail, and I gave her a hug. Then I straightened my shoulders and went into the kitchen, where I could hear Ariana moving about.

"Scrambled eggs?" she said over her shoulder.

"That would be great."

"Help yourself to coffee."

"Thank you."

Ah, we were so formal today. A finger of fire touched me as an image from last night flickered in my mind.

How should I play this? Not needy. That would drive Ariana away completely. Brittle sophistication wasn't me. Safest to imagine it was the same as a night with Chantelle, a lovely romp in the sheets, with no significant emotional entanglements. A subject for banter, not serious feelings.

She served the eggs, buttered the toast, and sat opposite me in the breakfast booth. We ate in silence for a few moments, then she put down her fork and for the first time this morning looked directly at me.

"Kylie, last night...It was a mistake."

"You're sorry it happened?"

The faintest of smiles touched her lips. "I'd be lying if I said I was sorry. Last night I needed someone."

"That's *such* a cliché."

Ariana blinked at me. "What?"

"Next you'll be saying it was the alcohol."

She sat back and regarded me with a quizzical expression.

I said, "Then I'll say to you, 'Are you playing hard to get?' and you'll say to me..." I gestured for her to fill in the words.

"I'm impossible to get."

"Excellent," I said. "You understand the cliché game very well."

I took a sour pleasure in the fact I'd disconcerted her. A feather of anger brushed me. Was Ariana expecting I'd behave like some young teenager caught up in the exciting rush of a first sexual infatuation? But then I realized I wasn't being fair. I'd asked myself in, and she'd accepted. There'd been no stipulation that she fall in love.

I looked up to find her watching me. "What are you thinking?" she asked.

Sliding out of the booth, I said, "I'm thinking I must be going. I've got a busy day ahead."

Ariana followed me to the door, a slight, puzzled frown on her face. "It was a lovely night, thank you," I said. "See you tomorrow."

She stood at the door and watched me drive away. As soon as I found a safe spot I pulled over to find a handkerchief to mop my eyes and blow my nose. My eyes kept filling with tears all the way home.

Once there, I hugged Julia Roberts, dashed cold water in my face, and called my aunt. "Aunt Millie, we're going for a drive to Santa Barbara. I'll pick you up in half an hour. And if you're not too sick of shopping, we can stop at the outlet stores."

"You're on!" said my aunt.

* * *

I didn't want to be first into Ariana's office for the scheduled Monday morning meeting. I couldn't think it would be anything but awkward for us to face each other without the buffer of other people being present.

When I finally went in, everyone but Ariana was chomping on doughnuts. "There's a chocolate one left, your favorite," Lonnie said to me. "Grab it fast before anyone else gets it."

It was totally ridiculous that his consideration over a stupid doughnut had tightened my throat. I snarled silently at myself, *Get a grip, Kylie.*

Sitting down next to Bob, I said brightly to him, "How's it going?"

He gave me an odd look. "OK, I suppose."

"If we can start," said Ariana, "I had a very interesting call early this morning from an investigative reporter at the *L.A. Times.* It seems the newspaper has kept under wraps the fact they're investigating the Church of Possibilities and, more specifically, Brother Owen. A series exposing the church is scheduled to run next month."

"How did he get to you?" Bob asked.

"When the reporter realized we were out there asking questions too, he wanted to know what we'd discovered. I said it was a Kendall & Creeling client involved and therefore confidential. I'll contact Nanette Poynter later to see if she's willing to cooperate with the *Times*. It's likely she will."

We discussed the impact this would have on my case. I didn't say much, just listened. Harriet had harsh words about the contract Alf and Chicka had signed with Lamb White.

"To sum up," Harriet said, "the terms of the contract are unconscionable. The morals clause will be triggered by anything Lamb White finds felonious or immoral. That covers a lot of ground. And perhaps even worse, as you suspected, Kylie, the Hartnidge brothers have inadvertently licensed Lamb White to hold the rights to all Oz Mob characters. That means, even if the Hartnidges aren't involved, the characters they've created can be used in any Lamb White movie or television production."

"So what would happen to the present Oz Mob movie," I asked, "if Alf and Chicka were arrested for opal smuggling?"

"All the rights would stay with Lamb White. They'd take over the project and freeze the brothers out."

"Crikey," I said, "can they really do that?"

"I imagine the Hartnidges can challenge this original contract on the grounds that it is unconscionable and unreasonable," Ariana said.

"If they don't pull off this movie, Alf and Chicka are close to broke," said Lonnie. He shook his head. "You've never seen such a financial mess. There's no way they'd be able to field a pack of top-flight lawyers, and that's what you'd need to take on Lamb White and the church."

"What about playing a waiting game?" said Bob. "We can hope the *L.A. Times* exposé will bring down the whole Church of Possibilities organization. Lamb White would fall too."

Harriet didn't agree with waiting. "It could be years. Brother Owen will fight with every resource he's got. In the meantime, the Hartnidge twins lose everything."

"A sting," I said. Everyone looked at me. "Let's set Lamb White up. Let *them* be caught with the opals and charged with smuggling. Alf and Chicka claim to know nothing about it, playing naive little Aussies who are victims of big business."

"Not a bad idea in theory," said Bob, "but how the hell do we pull it off?"

"Tami Eckholdt," I said. "She's the key."

CHAPTER TWENTY-TWO

"Tami?" I said into the receiver. "It's Kylie. You said to call."

"I did!" Her enthusiasm was disturbing.

"Tami, can we get together for a chat? I have this problem."

"I'd love that!"

It was two days after the Monday morning meeting. The paralyzing haze of unhappiness that had surrounded me had lifted as I plunged into the details of planning the sting.

I'd insisted we name our maneuver the Kookaburra Gambit. After all, COP's Lamb White had set the gambit up in the first place by filling Kelvin Kookaburras with stolen opals. What we would do now, if it all worked out, was boomerang the scheme right back to them.

I arranged to meet with Tami Eckholdt in a coffee shop. I was wired for sound, so Lonnie told me to pick a corner not too noisy and definitely not near the coffee machine.

I was there early to scope the place out. Tami arrived shortly afterward. Today she wore a very short, bilious green skirt and a tight yellow top. For myself, I'd ratcheted down the alluring factor with old baggy jeans and an overlarge denim shirt. I had a rather shabby canvas book bag sitting on the floor between my feet.

Even dressed like that, apparently I was Tami's cup of tea. "You look wonderful," she breathed, sitting at the little table I'd snaffled in a private corner. She put her hand on my knee.

"Thank you. You look wonderful too."

She leapt up, startling me. "I'll get the coffee. You stay here." She didn't ask how I liked my coffee.

Tami strode across the shop, bounced in place while waiting for her order, collected the overpriced cartons, then marched back to our table. That amount of energy was alarming, especially when she so obviously intended to expend some of it on me, if she got the chance.

"You said you had a problem, Kylie? I'd love to help, if I could."

"It's like this, Tami," I said, sounding deeply troubled, "Alf's given me these opals."

"Typical male." Her mouth twisted in disdain. "Men are always doing that, trying to buy sex with gifts. It's disgusting."

"The opals weren't a gift. There's lots of them, all loose stones. Not made up as jewelry. Alf asked me to keep them safe for him."

This was clearly an unwelcome shock for Tami. "Really?" she said. "Loose opals, you say?"

"Lots of them."

Tami chewed her lip. Her feet did a little dance under the table. She could have done with a glance at *The Complete Handbook's* advice on revealing body language.

"Where did they come from?" she said at last.

I did the looking-over-the-shoulder bit. "It's confidential, Tami. I don't know if I can tell even you…"

"Oh, you can tell me, Kylie. Trust me, you can."

"I don't know…" I looked pensive.

Tami put a comforting hand on mine. "I can see it's worrying you so much. Do share it with me. It'll help."

"True, my mum always says a worry shared is a worry halved."

Tami couldn't be less interested in Mum's take on life. "The opals, Kylie? Where did they come from?"

"They're lovely, and very valuable. Alf wouldn't tell me how much, but I know it's a lot of money."

She was getting impatient. "I'm sure. Where did you say he got them?"

"Alf found them in a crate of Kelvin Kookaburras Lamb White asked to be shipped from Australia." I dropped my voice. "Tami, he thinks *Lamb White* is smuggling opals."

"That's outrageous!" Tami's indignation was so obviously fake, I nearly smiled.

"What should I do with them?"

"What?"

It was obvious Tami wasn't sure how to respond at this point. I pressured her by saying, "I do need your advice." I reached down for the book bag. "What do I do with them?"

Tami stared at the bag with alarmed fascination. "You haven't got the opals *here*, have you?"

"I thought they were safer if I kept them with me."

The wheels in Tami's head were whirring, but not coming up with much. "I have to call someone," she said.

"At a moment like this?" I protested. "When I need your advice?"

Tami had whipped out a cell phone. "I'll be back in a moment." She scuttled out the door of the coffee shop, her face anxious. I watched as she carried on an urgent conversation, then she snapped the phone shut, trotted back inside, and sat down again. "Sorry about that. Business call."

"What should I do?" I sounded plaintive.

"Can I see them?"

I handed her the bag. She peered in, gaped at the opals lying tumbled in the bottom of the bag. "Jesus Christ!" This seemed an appropriate exclamation for the head of Lamb White.

"These came from the Kelvin Kookaburras at the Oz Mob office, is that right?" Tami's voice now had a steely note.

"Yes, but Alf thinks there may be opals in some other crates that haven't been opened yet. He's got the crates safe in storage."

Tami smiled at me. A counterfeit smile if I'd ever seen one. "Kylie, I want you to trust me."

"I want to, Tami, I want to."

"I'd like you to come with me. There's someone you need to meet."

"I don't want anyone else involved." I'd sharpened up my voice. "You see, Tami, I was thinking of keeping them."

Tami's jaw actually dropped. "Keeping the opals for yourself?"

I put on an expression of rat cunning. "Alf can't say anything, can he? The opals are what you call *hot*, isn't that the lingo? You'd get your share, if you'd help me."

That offer got a look of calculation from Tami. Then, frowning, she considered the possibilities. Really, she was transparent as glass. After a long pause, she said, "We could keep some of the opals. I guess no one would ever know."

I got obstinate. "I'm not taking this chance for *some* of the opals. I want all of them."

Tami tried to hide her fury with a smile. "Of course you do, but Brother Owen knows you have the opals. It'd be dangerous to cross him, but he'd never miss a few." She had another look in the bag. "Do you know which ones are worth the most?"

"That phone call you made—it was to Brother Owen, wasn't it?"

"He is my boss," Tami said defensively.

I took a handful of opals out of the bag and displayed them on the palm of my hand. "Look for ones with a shot of fire in them. They're worth the most."

Tami's face was a picture of greed. She picked several up and examined them. I murmured, "Each one is worth thousands."

"How many do you think we could take without it being noticed?"

"Maybe three each."

"Make it five or six." Tami slipped the opals she held into her pocket. "Now we go see Brother Owen. Hurry up and pick the ones you're keeping. He's waiting for us."

I selected several stones and put them in the hip pocket of my jeans. "Brother Owen shouldn't get the opals," I said resentfully. "They're not his."

Tami sniggered, not a nice sound. "They are, you know."

I did my dim, puzzled act. Tami looked at me with scorn. "You don't get it, do you, Kylie? Who do you think came up with the idea of planting the opals in the first place?"

"Not Brother Owen?" I said.

"Brother Owen. And they're going right back into the kookaburra toys, where Alf Hartnidge found them."

"It's something to do with the Oz Mob movie, isn't it? Alf told me he was worried about the morals clause."

Tami looked at me sharply. "What do you know about that?"

"Nothing much. I heard Alf and Chicka talking, that's all."

"Talking about the contract with Lamb White?" She leaned closer. "Tell me exactly what you heard them say."

"Gee, I don't know" I said vaguely. "It's not like I was really interested. I just caught a few words. Something about a legal challenge to the contract because some of the conditions were clearly unfair."

Obviously this was not welcome information. Tami muttered something under her breath, then startled me yet again by suddenly leaping to her feet. "Come with me."

I put on my mulish face. "No way." I clutched the canvas bag to my chest. "These are mine."

Tami looked around the coffee shop, possibly wondering if anybody would notice should she deliver a knockout blow, sling me over her shoulder, and carry me away. Since we'd already attracted the attention of a scruffy bloke at the table next to us, who'd been tapping away at a screenplay on his laptop, I decided my jaw was safe for the moment.

From her expression, Tami was struggling to find a way to persuade me to accompany her without actually slugging me. Apparently charm won, as she sat down again, put her elbows on the table, leaned forward, and said with warm sympathy, "I totally understand your hesitation, Kylie, but truthfully, I want what's best for you."

"Oh, yeah?" My skepticism was obvious.

"Kylie, don't be that way. You can trust me, truly you can. You have my word on that." A big, toothy smile flashed onto her face.

The Complete Handbook had a lot to say about identifying the lying smile. I'd paid attention, because in this town of perfect teeth, constant smiling was practically mandatory. I mean, why spend all that money if you're not going to flash your pearly whites?

I assessed Tami's smile, which was still at full force. My handbook noted that lying smiles last longer, and this one had been going on for some time. Phony smiles tend to use the bottom half of the face. This also checked out, as Tami's eyes remained flintlike while her teeth sparkled below. Third, a false smile is put together much more quickly than a genuine one, and disappears more rapidly. As I gazed at her, Tami's smile abruptly vanished.

"Brother Owen is not a patient man," she snapped. "He expects to see us—*and* the opals—soon. I told him we'd be leaving immediately. It's not wise to make him unhappy."

Charm was out. Bullying was in.

"So what can he do to me?" I shook the canvas bag for emphasis. "I've got the opals and he hasn't."

"I'd hate to see you come to harm."

I drew myself up. "Are you threatening me?"

The scruffy bloke had abandoned his screenplay and was openly staring at us. "Do you mind?" he said. "I'm creating here."

"Oh, *please*," said Tami, rolling her eyes. "*Creating!*"

"And *you'd* know?" sneered the scruffy bloke.

"As a matter of fact, I would." Tami declared. "I happen to run a major movie company."

Consternation filled his face. "Oh, shit!"

Tami smiled triumphantly—a genuine smile this time. "You've blown it, buddy."

"But I've got this surefire hit screenplay…"

Tami made a big show of ignoring him. "Where were we, Kylie?"

"You were threatening me."

"Threatening?" She tsk-tsked over that. "What I was doing was *warning* you. Brother Owen plays hardball." She reached over to give my hand a squeeze. "But we can manage this together and come out on top."

I pretended to ponder for a moment or two. "If I go with you, what's the deal?"

Tami's shoulders relaxed. She thought she had me, and all that was necessary now was to reel me in. "I'll tell you in the car. Trust me, it will be to your advantage."

"All right," I said, oozing reluctance. "But don't leave me alone with Brother Owen. He makes me nervous."

"I'll look after you, Kylie."

"You make me nervous too."

"I do?" This obviously pleased Tami. "Trust me, you have no reason to be anxious about me. I have only your best interests at heart."

The scruffy bloke gazed morosely after us as we exited the coffee shop.

CHAPTER TWENTY-THREE

Half a block down from the coffee shop was a handicapped parking zone. In it sat a huge white Mercedes sedan. "Lovely, isn't it?" said Tami. It burped discreetly as she unlocked the doors.

"I'd rather go in my car," I said. Lonnie had put a global positioning gizmo on it, so wherever I drove, the vehicle could be located.

"You'll be much more comfortable in mine."

"But my car's on a meter." I checked my watch. "And it's about the expire."

"Don't worry about it. Lamb White will pay the fine."

Inside, the Mercedes had that terrific new-car smell. I sank into the luxury of the leather seat as I watched Tami take the blue plastic sign announcing the driver was handicapped off the rearview mirror.

As she shoved it in the glove box, I said, "I didn't know you were handicapped."

"I'm not."

"So you're taking some handicapped person's spot?"

"They'll never miss it. Besides, my time is valuable. I can't waste precious minutes looking for somewhere to park."

The engine came to life with a well-mannered purr, and without indicating, Tami pulled out into the traffic. "Do you like this car?" she asked.

"It's OK."

Tami tossed off a laugh. "Just OK? This model is top of the line. One of the perks of working for Lamb White." She leaned over to put her hand on my thigh. Knees were bad enough. Now thighs? I repressed a quiver of horror.

With a meaningful little smile, accompanied by a thigh squeeze that hurt—she had fingers of steel—Tami said, "How would you like to join the Lamb White family, Kylie, as my personal assistant? A new car comes with the position."

"Dinkum? I'd get a Mercedes like this?"

This thought amused her. "I'm afraid these are reserved for top executives. Yours would be an entry level luxury sedan, or perhaps a mid-range SUV."

"I'll think about it." I looked around. "Where are we going?" She didn't answer.

Bob and Lonnie should be following the Mercedes. That was the plan if Tami insisted on using her car. I did a casual sweep of vehicles around us but couldn't see Bob's silver Toyota, or Lonnie's shabby Nissan. Of course that was the point—I wasn't supposed to be able to spot them. Still, it gave me a hollow feeling to think they might have lost me.

"We have to get our stories straight," Tami said. "Alf gave you these opals, and, worried that you could be involved in something illegal, you turned to me. Now, together, we've gone to Brother Owen for advice."

"But he was the one who planned the whole kookaburra scam in the first place."

"Don't mention that!" said Tami urgently. "Brother Owen mustn't know I've said anything to you about his being involved."

"You want me to lie?"

Tami gave me an exasperated glare. "Keep it simple. Alf gave you the opals. You didn't know what to do. You came to me. End of story."

We turned onto Rexford Drive. Obviously we were going to the French provincial house where the Lamb White barbecue had been held. I couldn't resist a look over my shoulder to see if any vehicle I recognized had followed us. None had. I had a sinking feeling something had gone wrong.

A middle-aged woman in a black dress opened the door for us. Brother Owen was waiting just inside. "Come in," he said, his manner solemn. I saw him eyeing my grubby canvas bag.

He led the way to a sumptuous study, lined with books and filled with heavy, dark furniture. Brother Owen ushered Tami and me to fat, wine-red leather chairs and seated himself opposite us. Giving me a small, avuncular smile, he said, "Tami tells me, Kylie, that Alf Hartnidge has given you a number of unset opals. It appears these have been smuggled into the States. This is a very serious situation."

Tami nodded a silent affirmation of the gravity of the circumstances.

"If the cops don't know anything about it, it isn't," I said.

Brother Owen leaned back in his chair. "I see. So you weren't thinking of going to the authorities?"

"I'm not sure what to do."

He shook his head regretfully, "It's hard to accept, but Alf's betrayed your trust, and mine too."

Tami shook her head, too, at the deceit of it all.

I put on a puzzled frown. "I don't get what you mean."

"It's clear to me Alf and Chicka arranged for the opals to be hidden in the kookaburra toys in Australia. Obviously they plan to sell them here. Now you've been implicated in this illegal activity. I'm afraid law enforcement won't believe your protestations of innocence. You're in a lot of trouble, my dear."

"I don't see why," I announced. "Alf said it was *you* who arranged for the opals to be put in the kookaburras."

Another regretful shake of his head. "After all I've done for Alf and Chicka Hartnidge. After all the opportunities they've been given."

"Shocking," murmured Tami.

Brother Owen gazed at the ceiling, as if calling for divine guidance. "As a man of God, I'll turn the other cheek, no matter how deep the betrayal, but still, the deceit breaks my heart."

"You'll turn them in?"

His attention snapped back to me. "Of course not. It's not my role to judge." Another ceiling glance. This bloke had that in common with Melodie. "There is a higher, heavenly court that ultimately Alf and Chicka must face."

"So what happens to the opals?" I asked, ever practical.

"You will be giving the opals to me." He put out his hand. "These precious stones will be used in the work of the Church of Possibilities. Thus, out of evil comes good."

"Amen," said Tami.

Ron Udell came into the room. With his soft, flabby body and rumpled clothes, he was as unappetizing as he'd been at the Oz Mob Burbank offices. "I got here as soon as I could." He scowled at me, then said to Brother Owen, "Did you check her out?"

"No need. Kylie came to me for counsel." A self-satisfied smile. "And I believe we've solved her little problem."

"You can't afford to be careless." Udell went to a drawer in the desk and took out some sort of electronic instrument. I had a fair idea what it was. He strode over to me, the instrument extended in his hand.

It beeped. "Christ! She's wired!"

Both Brother Owen and Tami leapt up, mouths agape. Brother Owen put his hands to his head. "Jesus! Jesus! What the fuck did I say?"

Ron Udell, not standing on ceremony, ripped open my shirt and grabbed the microphone attached to my bra. He smashed it with his heel. Then he searched me roughly. "It's a radio transmission to someone outside the building."

Brother Owen turned on Tami. "You stupid bitch! You brought her here!"

"It's not fair to blame me. You told me to, she said resentfully.

"Fuck," said Udell, his face ashen. "If it's the feds, we've had it."

Brother Owen seized my shoulders and shook me violently. "Who is it? The feds? Tell me!"

"It's Alf and Chicka," I got out.

He released me. "The Hartnidges?"

"They realized you were setting them up, so you could take over the whole Oz Mob operation. I said I'd help."

Ron Udell let out a sigh of relief. "The Hartnidges. We can handle them."

Brother Owen released his breath in a similar sigh. "Thank God."

"Alf and Chicka are right, aren't they?" I said. "You arranged to have the opals put in the Kelvin Kookaburras, didn't you?"

"Don't say anything to her," said Udell.

Brother Owen shrugged. "Who's she going to tell, and be believed?" He was visibly regaining his pompous self-importance, now that his panic had subsided.

"You're absolutely right," he said to me. "It was an ingenious scheme. The Oz Mob concept is an excellent one, but the Hartnidge brothers have no idea how to fully exploit it. I do. I'm sure they'll listen to reason and sign the rights over to Lamb White. If they play along, I'll make sure they get something for their trouble. If not…" His gesture condemned Alf and Chicka to the outer reaches.

"And you didn't have much overhead with the scam," I said, "since you used stolen opals."

He looked at me with sudden misgiving. "How did you know that?"

"They were stolen from Ralphie's Opalarium in Wollegudgerie."

"How did you know that?" he repeated.

"Oh, fuck," said Ron Udell, as the study door opened.

"Excuse me, sir," said the woman in the black dress. "These gentlemen—"

Four men in dark suits pushed past her. "Thank you. We'll take it from here."

CHAPTER TWENTY-FOUR

Lonnie was rightly pleased with himself. It had been his idea to wire me twice. Ron Udell had discovered the obvious transmitter and destroyed it. The second one, a tiny thing disguised as a button on my shirt, had continued to transmit everything that was said in the room.

Apart from that, Lonnie and Bob, staking out the coffee shop, had seen Tami arrive in her white Mercedes. After she'd gone in to meet me, Lonnie had casually stopped to tie his shoelaces next to her car so that he could surreptitiously fix a global positioning device to the vehicle. That meant they could follow us at a distance, without any worries they would lose me.

Ariana had handled the law-enforcement side, liaising with a friend high up in the LAPD and using a contact in the FBI to set up the arrests.

Brother Owen made bail, huffing his innocence of all charges, which included fraud, smuggling, extortion, and tax evasion. The *L.A. Times* published their series exposing the Church of Possibilities early, to coincide with the publicity.

Tami Eckholdt and Ron Udell were said to be cooperating fully with the authorities in their inquiries.

In Australia, Ralphie Bates had been arrested on the initial charge of insurance fraud.

With a compassionate thought for the unsuspecting casino operators, I'd put my Aunt Millie on a flight to Las Vegas.

Alf and Chicka Hartnidge were in talks with several industry executives with the view of having another movie studio take over the Oz Mob project.

At Kendall & Creeling, everything was back to normal. Buoyed by the possibility she'd still get to play Penny Platypus, Melodie was busy refining what she fondly believed to be an Aussie accent.

This had driven Fran to distraction. She and Melodie had a yelling match in the kitchen, and Harriet and I had to separate them.

Fran, snarling, marched off in one direction, Melodie, peeved, marched off in the other.

"I'd say Fran will blow her foofer valve if she doesn't look out," I said.

"Her what?" said Harriet.

"Foofer valve. It's just a saying, like you might remark that someone's gone berkers, and to watch out, because they're likely to blow a gasket...or a foofer valve."

Harriet looked at me dubiously. "If you say so," she said. She walked off, shaking her head.

Actually, there was something that wasn't back to normal at Kendall & Creeling. It was the way Ariana was treating me, as if I might suddenly embarrass her with some outpouring of inappropriate emotion.

I'd have to set her straight, so we could go back to the way we were before we'd made love. I tried not to think of that night too much, but images of us together in her bed jolted me when I least expected them.

I gave it some thought and decided it would be best to be direct. I'd approach this logically. After everyone had gone, I collected a writing pad and pen, and I took them into the kitchen where Julia Roberts was dining on chicken.

"How's this, Jules?" I said. I read out: "Ariana, I hope you don't think I took that night with you too seriously. It was lovely, but just a one-night stand."

Julia Roberts stopped eating and looked at me.

"You're right, Jules. That makes Ariana seem cheap, as if she's just in it for sex. But then again, what's wrong with that? Sex is a good thing, don't you think?"

Julia Roberts went back to her chicken. I went back to my writing pad.

"OK, how about this: Ariana, we're business partners. I don't want to imperil that relationship."

Imperil wasn't the right word. *Endanger? Put at risk?*

I tried again. "Ariana, we're business partners. I don't want to put that relationship at risk." I looked to Julia Roberts for help. "Professional relationship would read better, do you think?"

I altered it. Tried it out on Julia Roberts again. She was tough to please. Back to the drawing board.

In the morning I practiced in my bathroom, watching my facial expressions carefully. *The Complete Handbook* did say that practiced liars could fool almost anybody, and I was nothing if not practiced at this point.

Ariana came in early. I waited until she had her coffee and had disappeared into her office. I put my head around the door and said, "Could I have a word with you?"

"Of course. Come in."

She was wearing the outfit I liked best on her—tailored black top, black pants, and high-heeled boots.

I shut the door behind me, sat down opposite her and said, before I could chicken out, "Ariana, we're business partners. I want you to know there's no way I'd put that professional relationship at risk."

So far, so good. At this point in my mental rehearsals of our conversation, she was supposed to respond with some remark, but Ariana remained silent, looking at me with what seemed sadness in her eyes.

She was sorry for me. I *hated* that. OK, I'd get out of this with as much dignity as I could.

I had my next line ready. This would reassure her. I saw the words as if printed in the air: *Ariana, as far as I'm concerned, the other night never happened.*

She was waiting for me to speak. I heard myself say, "Ariana, I adore you."

"I know," she said.

Bella Books, Inc.

Women. Books. Even Better Together.

P.O. Box 10543
Tallahassee, FL 32302

Phone: 800-729-4992
www.bellabooks.com